THE NIGHT CHICAGO DIED
A Justice Security Novel
By
T. M. Bilderback

I0549696

For Shea

You've been my friend for over thirty years
And are still teaching this old dog some new tricks

Author's Note:

Welcome to the new edition of The Night Chicago Died – A Justice Security Novel. *This novel was previously published in Kindle Worlds, was exclusive to Kindle Worlds, and teamed Justice Security with another fictional world by another author. With the demise of Kindle Worlds, rights to the story reverted back to me. The author whose characters were teamed with mine told me that I could re-work my story without his characters. I've done that.*

If you've purchased the story when it was in Kindle Worlds, you basically already have the story. It hasn't changed. The only changes have been to introduce my own characters that work with the Chicago Police Department. So, if you already have the story in its old form, it's not too late to ask for a refund.

If you haven't read the story because of that retailer's exclusivity of the story, you are in for one slam-bang ride, as Justice Security's mortal enemy, Esteban Fernandez, attempts to take over Chicago, in this eighth story in the Justice Security series.

You'll also meet Lieutenant Mickey Rooney. She is no relation to the actor, and her actual given name is Michelle. Her current partner is Detective First Grade Sam Tanner, and her old partner, now a private detective, is Manny Salazar. I like these characters, and, at some point, I plan to tell the story of the Corn Flakes Killer...but not for a little while.

So, turn the page or swipe your finger on the screen, and let's get this show started!

T. M. Bilderback

Chapter 1

Tim "Skanky" Sanders danced from foot to foot, waiting for his supplier to show up. It was a cold, windy night for early November, and snow was forecast for overnight...three inches. Not really worth mentioning for Chicago, but Skanky came from a city further south, and wasn't used to Chicago winters. Even after five years, Skanky was having trouble keeping warm.

Jesus Christ, *when is he coming?* thought Skanky to himself. *He said ten. Ten PM, and it's five past now! I got people waiting for some new shit, and this damn street corner is damn cold!*

Tim Sanders sold things. Meth, heroin, coke, pot, uppers, downers, oxys, hydros, Xanax, Valiums, over-the-counter cold medicines (for the do-it-yourselfers), even aspirin, if somebody wanted it. Skanky didn't care. He was everybody's street dealer. Sometimes, he sold to cops, and he sold to them at a fair price. It kept him from getting busted.

Sanders got the nickname "Skanky" from his days selling in Hooker Hollow in that southern city. Hooker Hollow was really Third Street on any map, but city locals called it Hooker Hollow because of the business conducted there. The hookers along Hooker Hollow all bought their shit from Sanders, but they all agreed that he was too "skanky" to have sex with...unless they needed what Sanders had and were a little short of money. Then, they'd pay Skanky with a quick blowjob or a fast roll in the hay, depending on the cost of what they needed. Sometimes, what the hookers wanted was a little more expensive than what the hookers had to offer, so Skanky came up with another idea. Customers of the hookers often talked about things during pillow talk...things that could be used. Sold, even.

Skanky became a seller of information. Most of the hookers became very adept at getting information from their clientele, along with their clients' names, and they would pass it all along to Skanky in exchange for what they needed.

Skanky's sex life dried up, but the money poured in like water.

Skanky sold information to anyone about anything.

Women began looking to Skanky to find out if their men had been paying for what they could have had at home. Men looked to Skanky to find out the same information about their women. Skanky sold information to private investigators – Nicholas Turner was a good customer, along with some of the people from Justice Security. Cops would pay for information about a person of interest, and Skanky sold it to them. Ten minutes later, Skanky would try to find that person of interest, and sell them the tip that the cops were looking for them.

One type of information never left his lips. He never ratted out the hookers that traded with him. Pimps would come around, asking if their hookers were holding out on them, and Skanky would always answer that they weren't. Since the hookers were run by these pimps, and the pimps were run by the Giambini crime family, Skanky did what he could to protect his sources of information.

Finally, five years ago, Skanky was given a piece of information by one of his most dependable hookers. One of the tidbits of information he had sold to the cops had thwarted a job that the Giambinis were about to do. Mickey Giambini himself had ordered that Skanky be killed.

As soon as the hooker had walked away, Skanky had walked away, too. He didn't even stop to pack. He got into his rattletrap car, stopped to retrieve most of his cash from his bank's safety deposit box, and drove north. He finally settled in Chicago. He felt confident that Mickey Giambini would not bother with him as long as he stayed there.

It didn't take long for Skanky to begin peddling drugs again. It was how he started out, and it was decent money. The crime families in Chicago were much more calm and businesslike...not unpredictable like Mickey Giambini.

A few days later, through a phone call to a friend, Skanky found out that the hooker that had given him the information about Giambini's intentions had been beaten to death.

Skanky now stayed away from selling information. A guy could get killed that way.

This evening, Skanky had received a phone call from the Tinker. Tinker was his main supplier, and had told Skanky to meet him at ten o'clock on this lonely corner on the South Side.

"You sound a little out of breath, Tinker," said Skanky. "You okay?"

Tinker's voice sounded strained. "Yeah, I'm okay, man...just a little winded from the stairs."

"Okay, Tinker, I'll be there."

Skanky looked at his watch. *Okay, it's ten past now. I'll wait another five minutes, then I'm outta here.*

A hand touched the sleeve of his coat, and Skanky jumped, yelling, "Hey!" He whirled around to see who had touched him.

A man and a woman, both customers, were standing behind Skanky.

"I'm sorry we scared you, man," said the man. He and the woman were both dressed in what used to be snappy designer clothing, but had been neglected and misused since they had both become his customers. "We followed you. We're looking for a little quartz...we need it pretty bad."

The woman nodded her agreement with what the man was saying. "We have money."

Skanky shook his head. "I'm dry right now. I can't help you, but...I'm supposed to meet my supplier here any minute now. He won't stop if he sees anybody else here." He thought for a minute. "Tell you what – why don't you two go hide in the alley there." He pointed to the alley directly behind them. "Get behind the dumpster. You can watch, but if he sees you, he probably will kill you!" *He wouldn't,* thought Skanky, *but he might steal my business. Prick.* "Then, when he's gone, I'll fix you right up."

The couple nodded, desperation showing in their faces and their eyes. They turned briskly, went into the alley, and got behind the dumpster.

Not bad. The only reason I can see them is because I know they're there.

As Skanky completed this thought, headlights began coming down the deserted side street. A long, sleek, black limousine pulled to a stop under the streetlight, with the back door even with Skanky.

What the hell is this?

The limo driver, a Hispanic man, got out and opened the rear door. His passenger got out of the limousine. He was average height and well-dressed, with a tailored suit, neatly trimmed hair and beard, and manicured nails. His hair was mostly gray, with a few spots of black showing at the temples and in a couple of places in his beard. His complexion was dark beige, and his eyes were black, and rarely blinked.

"*Buenos noches,*" said the well-dressed man.

"I don't speak Spanish, buddy," replied Skanky. He couldn't stop staring at the man's eyes. Skanky thought that the man might blink sometime, but, if he did, Skanky couldn't see it.

"Then I will speak English, so that you may understand me." The man wore light goatskin gloves, and began taking them off as he talked. "You are the one they call 'Skanky'?"

"Who wants to know?"

The man moved his head in acknowledgement. "I do, *senor.*"

"What are you, a cop or something?"

"No, I am not an officer. Not in this country."

"Yeah, well, look, it's been nice talking to you, but I got an appointment..."

"Yes, I know." The man put his gloves into his coat pocket. "Your appointment is with me."

Skanky eyed the man from head to toe. "You aren't the Tinker."

The man smiled broadly. The smile was almost a rictus, and Skanky thought this man had a close resemblance to a shark. It unnerved him, but he wouldn't let it show.

"No, *senor,* I am not the Tinker. Do you know who I am?"

Skanky, curious now, shook his head. "Haven't got a clue."

The well-dressed man reached inside his coat as he spoke. "*Me llamo es Esteban Fernandez.*"

At first, Skanky didn't recognize the name. But, as the seconds wore on, and the file cabinets inside his slow-moving brain opened, realization came to him.

This man was the insane Mexican drug cartel leader that carried the rank of General in his home country.

This was the man responsible for wiring the championship boxing match back in his old city with explosives. Had they exploded, thirty thousand people would have either died or been injured.

This was the man that built a nightclub that was really a Venus flytrap, sprung to try to capture Joey Justice and Misty Wilhite, and that killed dozens of people, including the mayor.

This was the only man that Mickey Giambini feared.

This man was facing him now, smiling with a predator's grin.

Skanky's bladder let go as his fear grew into a living thing.

"So you see, Skanky, I have come to Chicago to...organize things. You understand, of course. And I no longer require your services." Fernandez drew a gun from his coat and shot Skanky three times through the heart.

As Fernandez fired the third shot, and Skanky was falling to the ground, a taxi turned the corner into the deserted street. Fernandez turned to face the taxi.

The taxi driver quickly realized what was happening, even as Fernandez was aiming his gun at the passing vehicle. The driver began muttering, "*ohshitohshitohshit.*" He floored the gas pedal, and began weaving back and forth across the narrow street, trying to leave the area quickly with his life intact.

It was enough. Fernandez had fired seven rounds at the retreating taxi, but missed the driver. The taxi turned left at the first opportunity, and the driver used his cell phone to call the police.

"*Hijo de puta!*" shouted Fernandez.

The limousine driver, Felix Juarez, said, "Come, Esteban. He will call the *policia.* We must go now."

"Yes. Again, Felix, you are correct. We have much to do."

As the limousine drove away, Skanky's two customers came out from behind the dumpster and stepped cautiously out of the alley. They were holding hands tightly, staring at the cooling, unmoving body.

They were still standing there as the first two black-and-whites arrived.

Chapter 2

The black-and-whites had already taped off the area surrounding the body when I got to the scene. A few brave souls had come outside in the cold, windy night to stare at the dead man lying on the sidewalk.

Maybe they were hoping he would sit up and say, "April Fool!"

As I eased my 1998 Beetle to the curb and parked behind a taxi, I wondered why tonight was so busy. This was the third shooting that we'd been called to. All of them were street dealers.

You'd think the cold would keep people inside.

My partner, Detective First Class Sam Tanner, had gotten here first, and was talking to a couple of people that were holding hands and huddling close together on the sidewalk, inside the "Crime Scene" tape. I checked the cord that held my star to make sure that it hadn't frozen and broken off. It was still intact. I was a little disappointed.

I still hadn't taken the time to buy a new winter coat, and my London Fog trench coat over my blazer still didn't keep me warm. Add the slight limp from the almost healed bullet wound in my leg – compliments of the Corn Flakes Killer – and I was a little on the moody side.

I passed under the line and stopped to look at the body. A uniformed officer that I didn't know was standing guard, making sure that the body remained dead. The Medical Examiner hadn't arrived yet. With two other bodies, it looked like it might be a while before he *did* arrive.

I lifted the tarp that one of the officers had used to cover the body. Three shots to the heart, all less than an inch apart, in a perfect triangle. Even at close range, that was some fancy shooting. And the wounds and spacing were identical to the other two victims.

I put down the tarp and caught my partner's attention. He said something to the couple, and then walked over to me.

"What took you so long, Mickey? You stop for ice?"

"Don't let the chattering teeth fool you. I'm as warm as a convenience store pizza right now."

"Clearly, you haven't been to Tony's Pizzeria lately. I don't think their pizzas are warm even straight from the oven."

I indicated the victim. "Do we know who he is?"

Sam shook his head, jowls looking a bit like Jello as his head moved. Tiny icicles had formed in his salt-and-pepper moustache from the moisture in his breathing. "I haven't looked for ID because the ME hasn't gotten here yet. But, according to the two witnesses, the victim is Skanky Sanders."

"I'm supposed to know who that is?" I asked.

"I called it in. If it is Sanders, he's a street dealer. Been busted a couple of times, never prosecuted. Evidence seemed to disappear both times."

I knew what that meant. It meant that this guy sold to a few cops. And they kept him out of trouble in exchange for low prices. I shook my head.

"Witnesses?" I asked.

"We got lucky on this one. We got three. Those two," he pointed at the huddled couple, "saw the whole thing, and heard one of the two men say the name 'Esteban'. 'Esteban' called the other man 'Felix'." He pointed to the taxi. "The taxi driver drove by as the shooting happened. The perp shot at the taxi several times, but missed the driver. His description of the shooter matches the couple's."

"Why were those two out?" I asked as I pointed to the couple.

"Sanders was their dealer. They were looking to score a little meth."

I noticed their clothes. At one time, they had been expensive and stylish. Now, they were shabby and worn. Meth does that to a person. It lures you in, chews you up, and spits you out as a rotten mess.

I tried not to look too intimidating as I walked over to speak to the couple. I had decided not to be too "authoritative" as I spoke with them. Always the helpful cop. Yep, that's me.

"Hi, folks. My name is Lieutenant Rooney. Call me Mickey."

The man snickered. "You're kidding, right?"

I sighed. This was getting old. I took my badge case from around my neck, and showed both of them my official ID card. Lieutenant Mickey Rooney, CPD. Short for Michelle, but I wasn't telling them that.

"Any relation to the actor?" asked the man.

I sighed again. "No relation."

"Wow," said the woman. "I bet you get a lot of jokes about being called Mickey."

"Let me put it this way," I replied. "You can't come up with a joke that I haven't heard."

The man snickered again.

"Could I have your names?"

"I'm William, and this is my wife, Deborah," said the man.

"Last names?"

"Glick."

"Sanders was your dealer?"

The two exchanged worried glances.

"I'm not looking to make a bust, or to make your lives harder. I just need some questions answered." I looked from William to Deborah. "You have my word."

William looked into my eyes for a moment. I could see that he believed me. "Yeah, he was our dealer."

"How did you happen to be here with him?"

"We talked to him earlier. He said that he was dry, but that he could help us a little later. He said he was supposed to meet his supplier," said William.

"Yeah, so we followed him," said Deborah. "We wanted to get our stuff fresh off the cart."

I looked at her. "Is it that bad?"

They both nodded. "It's getting pretty bad right now."

"When we're done, if you'd like me to, I'll take you to a place that will help you. The City provides assistance for people that want to stop using." I let that sink in for a few seconds. "Now, what happened after you followed Sanders?"

"He said that his supplier was supposed to be there any minute. He told us to go into the alley and hide behind the dumpster. He said that his supplier would kill us if he saw us," said William.

"We saw the whole thing," said Deborah. "A black limousine pulled up in front of Skanky, and the driver opened the door for this guy. The guy talked to Skanky a little bit."

"The guy was Hispanic," added William. "I can't narrow it down any more than that."

"What did they talk about?" I asked.

William wrinkled his brow. "Skanky told the guy that he had an appointment, and told the Hispanic guy to beat it. The Hispanic guy said that Skanky's appointment was with him. Skanky said something about him not being the Tinker, whoever that is. Then the Hispanic guy asked if Skanky knew who he was, and Skanky said he didn't. Then the guy said something in Spanish. I think he said his name, because the sentence ended with Esteban Fernandez."

"Yeah, then this guy Esteban pulled out a gun and shot Skanky three times," said Deborah.

"We saw the taxi drive by, and this Esteban turned around and fired several times at the taxi. He must have missed. The limo driver told Esteban that they must go, because the taxi driver would call the police. Esteban agreed with the limo driver, and called him 'Felix'," said William. "They drove away after that."

"Did you get the license number?" I asked.

They both shook their heads.

"Thank you for your help. Please stay here a little longer, and I'll get you to that clinic."

Both Glicks thanked me.

Sam and I walked a short distance away.

"Any of those names ring a bell?" I asked my partner.

Sam was thinking. "I've heard the name Tinker...he's maybe a low-level supplier. The other two...something about Esteban Fernandez rings a bell, but I don't know why."

"Same here. I can't place it, though." I shivered. "Where's the taxi driver?"

"Sitting in his taxi."

Warmth. I thought it was time to question the taxi driver, and it might take some time. A long, warm time.

I walked to the cab, opened the front passenger seat, and climbed in. Sam climbed into the roomier back seat. The temperature inside the cab approached summertime. I basked in the heat for a few seconds, while the taxi driver argued over a CB radio with his dispatcher.

"No, I can't just leave," the driver was saying into the microphone. "I don't want the cops to arrest me."

"I'm telling you, if anyone shot up that cab, it's coming out of your pocket. And if you don't get rolling soon, you'll be out of a job," said the voice of the driver's dispatcher.

"What's your dispatcher's name?" I asked, before the driver could press the transmit key again.

"Lou. Lou Mitchell," said the taxi driver.

"Your name?"

"Tony Fisher."

I pressed the transmit key. "Am I speaking to Lou Mitchell?"

A few seconds passed. "This is Lou. Who the hell is this?"

I keyed the mike again. "This is Lieutenant Rooney, Chicago Police Department, Violent Crimes Division. Lou, I just overheard a conversation you had with my witness, Tony Fisher." I let go of the transmit key and said to Sam, "Hey, will you call one of those uniforms over?"

Sam rolled down a window and motioned one of the uniforms over. When the uniform reached the taxi, I rolled down my window so that the officer could hear what I was saying.

I pressed the transmit key. "Lou, you just urged my witness to leave the scene of a crime. You also have threatened to extort money from him for damages to this taxi that occurred beyond his control. Since insurance is required on all cabs in this city, the damage is covered. I can only guess that you want to pocket some of this driver's hard-earned pay for your own use, while collecting from the insurance company. That's attempting to commit insurance fraud.

"I'm sending Officer..." I squinted to read his name tag. "...Petrie over to your office right now. He'll be arresting you for obstruction of justice and attempted insurance fraud. I want you to stay right where you are." I let go of the key, and spoke to Officer Petrie. "Go over there and scare the pants off that guy, if he stays put. Don't officially arrest him, but cuff him, and make sure that anyone in the garage sees that he's handcuffed. Hang around with him for half an hour, then take the cuffs off of him. Say you've spoken with me and talked me out of arresting him. If he's gone, come back here and see if you can help." Petrie smiled broadly, happy to comply with my little joke.

I rolled up the window and listened to Tony and my partner laughing.

"I'll be very surprised if Lou is still at work when Petrie gets there," I said to Tony. "But, I bet he stays off your back."

Shaking his head and laughing, Tony said, "Thank you, Lieutenant Rooney. After being shot at, I needed the laugh."

"I know what you mean. Do you feel up to telling me what you saw?"

"Yeah, sure. Keep in mind, I was passing by. It happened pretty quick." Tony closed his eyes. "Hold on, I'm playing it back."

I looked at him.

"Before you ask, it's my way of recalling things. I close my eyes, and replay things in my mind. I can recall all sorts of things when I do that." He was quiet for a moment. "I turned the corner as the shooter was firing a shot. The man he shot was falling. The shooter's eyes actually met mine, and I somehow knew that he was going to start shooting at me. He turned, and I floored the gas pedal and began zig-zagging back and forth across the street."

"Did you see enough to get a description of the shooter?"

Eyes still closed, Tony said, "Dark complexion, almost like he tans a lot. Mostly gray hair, and a mostly gray beard, trimmed. Nice overcoat...long. London Fog, or another expensive brand, but not a light jacket – more like a thick trench coat, with a charcoal muffler. No hat. Had the gun in his right hand." He opened his eyes. "That's it. That's all I can remember."

I was impressed. I couldn't do what this man just did, even if I'd had more time to study the scene.

"Amazing!"

Tony smiled softly. "You'd be surprised what you can remember when you're being shot at."

I knew. But I wasn't going to tell Tony that.

I told Tony that the taxi would have to stay here until the lab people were through with it. The shooter had hit the taxi's trunk at least twice, and we would need the evidence. I told Tony that he was free to go, if he wanted to.

"I think I'll go home, Lieutenant," said Tony. "I'm a little shook up."

I thanked him, and gave him one of my cards in case he remembered something else. We had his address if we needed him.

Sam and I reluctantly climbed out of the taxi. I noticed two things immediately. One, the M. E. had arrived and had lifted the tarp to check out the victim, and, two, it was snowing.

Dalton McFee, goatee glistening with sparkles from the snow, put the tarp back over the victim. He said to us, "Officially, I can only say that death appears to be by gunshot. Unofficially, I can say that the same shooter did this one. Looks like somebody's executing street dealers, and is using a nine-millimeter."

One of the uniforms brought over a handheld radio. "Lieutenant, for you. There's another one."

"What the *hell?*" I said, as I took the radio.

DETECTIVE TORY MASTERSON from Narcotics met us at the scene of the fourth killing. He was talking on his cell phone when Sam and I arrived, while uniforms guarded the door.

"Well, it completely blows our case, that's what it means! Three months' work gone, just like that!" Masterson said forcefully. "Tinker was the only link to the people above him!" He listened for a moment, then said, "I already knew his three street dealers, and they're dead, too!" He noticed us standing at the open door to the apartment. "Sir, Lieutenant Rooney is here. Yes, sir. I'll tell her, sir." He disconnected the call, walked over, and shook hands with us.

Masterson had once been one of my people, back when he was a Detective/ Third. He had transferred to Narcotics after showing that he had a talent for undercover work. Now, as a Detective/First, he was lining up a lot of busts, and rumored to be on the fast track to Lieutenant. He was married, and I had heard that he had a new baby boy.

"Sorry, Lieutenant, that was Captain Phillips," said Masterson. "He said to tell you that I am officially yours until we solve these killings."

I grinned. "Glad to have you, Tory. I'll let Captain Baker know. He'll be happy to have you. And congratulations on the new baby!"

"So who's the victim this time, Masterson?" asked Sam.

Masterson led us over to the victim, who looked to be in his fifties, with salt-and-pepper hair. He had been tied to a kitchen chair, naked. It was obvious that he'd been tortured before he was killed. There were several shallow knife slashes, calculated to bleed and hurt, and an empty bottle of rubbing alcohol sat on the floor beside the chair. It looked as if the alcohol had been poured onto the knife wounds, but the M.E. would have to verify that. The cord from a lamp was also beside the chair. It was still plugged into the wall socket, and the plastic insulation had been stripped from the other end, exposing the copper wiring inside. There were a few marks on the body showing that the electricity had been applied, including on the victim's testicles. A cloth had been stuffed into his mouth, and then his mouth was duct taped closed. But, cause of death was probably the three small bullet holes in the victim's chest, probably through the heart, and arranged in a triangle.

"The vic's name was William Joseph Smith, also known as 'The Tinker'. At one time, he was a clock repairman - tinkered with old antique clocks, and that's how he earned his nickname," said Masterson. "The last few years, he's been a low level supplier."

I exchanged a look with Sam. That's where we'd heard the Tinker's name.

"Any idea who supplied him?" I asked.

Masterson shook his head. "No, we didn't get that far in yet." He pointed at the alcohol and the lamp cord. "But I'll bet you five bucks that whoever did this knows. I've got a couple of uniforms knocking on doors, asking the neighbors if they heard or saw anything, but chances are slim."

"We have a description of the shooter," I said. "We have witnesses." We told Masterson what we had learned at the last shooting. When I said the name 'Esteban Fernandez', Masterson whistled.

"Why the whistle?" I asked. "That name is familiar, but I can't place it."

"We got trouble, Lieutenant," said Masterson. "Fernandez carries the rank of General in Mexico, but he's also the biggest drug cartel leader to ever raise his ugly head in that country. Let me tell you what he did in a city down south..."

Masterson filled us in on what Fernandez had done. When he got to the part about the boxing match and the arena, I snapped my fingers. "John said something about that a few months ago! Turned out, the challenger was delaying the fight so that the bomb could be found and defused!" Masterson nodded, and told us more. I started getting a chill along my spine.

Masterson started ticking off points on his fingers. "One, you got a Mexican drug cartel leader in Chicago. Two, he's violent. Three, he's insane, which makes him very unpredictable. And, four, he's Federal."

Cops are very territorial about jurisdiction, and when I heard 'Federal', I cringed inwardly...but with a twinge of relief. "What do you mean by 'Federal'?" I asked.

"Narcotics got a bulletin from the FBI," answered Masterson. "It said that if we ever heard that this Fernandez showed up in our city that we were to notify them immediately. I guess it went out all over the country."

"Then we'll tell Captain Baker, and let him notify the Fibbies," I said. "One less thing we have to worry about."

Chapter 3

Justice Security, Incorporated owned its own building on a tree-lined street in a better part of the city. The six-story aboveground edifice occupied a large portion of a city block, with parking areas for visitors, and a landscaped, park-like green area on its south side. The building itself was constructed of three-foot-wide reinforced concrete walls. Each window was made of thick bulletproof glass, including the visitors' entrance door. The building extended six floors underground. The bottom three underground floors were used as a vehicle storage area, and housed various armor-plated and bullet resistant vehicles to be used as protective equipment for transporting and defending employees or clients. The next underground level was the armory. All types of weapons were stored in the climate-controlled armory, from revolvers and automatic pistols, to mortars, to surface-to-air missiles and launchers, and various armor-piercing weapons. Enough weaponry and ammunition were stored in the armory to take down a small country's government, should they be hired for such a thing...and they had done so, twice, a couple of years ago under an ultra-classified government contract. The floor above the armory was records storage. This floor contained the paper files, computers, data storage, and research areas needed for executing and completing client contracts. The final underground level was the garage for employee parking, and was accessed by a ground-level entrance contained by a thick, heavy steel door embedded into the concrete walls of the building.

At ground level, the first floor contained the reception area, the cafeteria, building security, the medical facility, and visitors' lounge. The second and third floors were occupied by employee offices, conference rooms, smaller meeting rooms, and clerical services, along with the employee gym. The fourth floor housed executive offices and the situation room. The fifth floor was for guest housing, and the top floor contained residential apartments for the top level people of the company. The roof of the building had a helicopter pad, equipped with two armor-reinforced, stealth-equipped, black ops helicopters always ready to fly at a moment's notice. The company also owned two private jets and two large cargo planes, which were housed at a private airfield just south of the city.

Justice Security had been formed a few years earlier by four college friends, who remained the directors and sole stockholders of the company.

Joey Justice, after whom the company was named, was a nondescript man. Standing at five feet ten inches, he had dark hair and intense brown eyes that usually missed nothing. He had founded the company with the premise of providing security services tempered with justice, as his name implied. He was very much in love with the lady in his life, who was also one of the cofounders of the company.

Misty Wilhite, the lady of Joey's life, stood five feet five. She had shoulder-length auburn hair, with green eyes. She was extremely attractive, but she had a punch that could drop a person twice her size. She, too, was very much in love with Joey, and shared his belief of security and justice. They had not married yet, but had just become engaged.

Dexter Beck was the resident computer nerd. Standing one inch taller than Misty, Dexter was consistently underestimated by antagonists. Understanding usually followed, because Dexter also was a martial arts master, utilizing several methods of self-defense. The security and computer systems used by Justice Security were created, programmed, and maintained by Dexter.

Percival "King Louie" Washington was the fourth founding member of Justice Security. Louie stood four inches over six feet, and had a very imposing muscular build. He also was very intelligent and street-smart. His skin was the color of a chocolate bar, and he kept his head shaved. The other three founding members had nicknamed him "King Louie" in their first year of college because of his unfortunate facial resemblance to the cartoon character in the Jungle Book movie. It wasn't racial, and Louie knew it...just like if he had had a big nose, they would have nicknamed him "Baloo". Besides, anything was better than his given name of Percy.

Recent additions to the partners included Jessica Queen, the former executive secretary to the four partners. Her immediate replacement as executive secretary, Patti Hoehn, had been tortured, killed and mutilated by Esteban Fernandez, who had caught her on the street snapping photos during the company's first encounter with him. Patti's replacement, Turk Wendell, was a huge, hulking man, who was surprisingly adept at performing secretarial duties.

Another addition to the partners had been Dexter Beck's right hand person, Megan Fisk Beck. She had led an attempted pre-emptive attack on Fernandez, and had gotten wounded in the process. She and Dexter had eloped, and were happily married newlyweds.

Every morning at nine, the partners gathered in the situation room to discuss current and upcoming events. This way, they kept up with all company business in case someone else had to step in and take over quickly.

This morning, right after the alarm clock shrilled its urgent seven o'clock wake-up call, Joey's private cell phone rang. He wiped his eyes, looked at the caller, and answered.

"Marcus Moore, don't you ever sleep?" said Joey into the phone. Misty stirred beside him, then turned over to face Joey. Sleep was still in her eyes.

Marcus Moore was Justice Security's FBI liaison. Marcus had been instrumental in getting Justice Security's top secret contract with the United States Government, guaranteeing a large amount of money plus expenses to the security company...but, to earn the money, they had to bring down Esteban Fernandez. And the contract specified that it be done with full governmental deniability, of course, and no on-the-record help by any government agency. Expense money would be funneled to them on the Q.T. by Marcus.

Justice Security had been given this contract because of events at *Wham!* nightclub. It had been secretly owned by Fernandez, and, in reality, had been a trap meant to capture Joey and Misty. The trap had sprung, but had only captured Joey and four "grunts" inside. Joey had found a hiding place, and had stayed hidden until the partners outside had found a way to break in. One grunt and several dozen innocent people had died during that escapade, both inside and outside. Only quick action by Tony Armstrong, Patty Ferguson, and Brandon King, with help from Channel 7 news reporter Miriam Apple and her cameraman, Steve, had saved many people inside the club from being slaughtered.

At the same time that the trap in the club had been sprung, the almost-deserted Justice Security building had been penetrated by a deep undercover assassin working for Fernandez. This agent had been dating Louie, and no one had suspected a thing. She had decimated the ranks of the people that had been left inside the locked-down building. Only Jessica had survived, along with Mark Haase, the desk "grunt" on the night shift.

After all of that, certain powerful people inside the government decided that it was time to hire someone to bring this insane Mexican general down...someone that could move quickly both inside the U.S. and in other countries.

Marcus had received a promotion to Section Chief from the FBI, and was now head of the city's satellite office. He also had certain other duties, including "unofficially assisting" Justice Security as needed. He could also deputize them as temporary field agents, if he felt that deputizing them would speed any investigation.

"Good morning, Sunshine!" Marcus replied to Joey. "At least I waited until your alarm went off before I called."

Joey turned to meet Misty's eyes as he answered. "You even disturbed the lady sleeping beside me." He leaned over and kissed her. As he settled back onto his pillow, she smiled at him and mouthed, "I love you."

Joey silently mouthed it back.

"I bet she's even more beautiful when she wakes up," said Marcus. "I've wound up waking up with a few that made me want to turn into a coyote, so that I could gnaw my arm off to keep from waking them up."

Joey chuckled as he sat up on the edge of the bed. Misty padded naked across the bedroom, heading for the bathroom to brush her teeth and start their shower running.

"Okay, Marcus, why the early call?"

"I just wanted to let you know that I'm coming to the nine o'clock this morning."

Joey yawned broadly. "Why? What's up?"

"Before I answer, will everyone be there?"

"You know they will."

"I mean, in person...not electronically."

"No, Jessica is in Los Angeles, soothing the ruffled feathers of a paranoid Oscar-winning actress."

"Damn! How secure will her connection be?"

"How secure do you want it, Marcus?"

"As secure as it can be, Joey. What I have for you is top secret."

"HIT ME, MEGAN," SAID Dexter.

"No."

"Come on, hit me!"

"No!"

"Why not?"

Megan Fisk Beck turned to look at her husband. "I've played this game too much with you, Dexter Beck! You know darn well I'm not fast enough to hit you."

"Oh, honey, please? This might be the day. You won't know until you try."

Almost faster than the human eye could follow, Megan feinted with a right cross. Dexter moved to the left to avoid it, and barely missed being caught by Megan's left uppercut.

"Whoa!" said Dexter in surprise.

Megan smiled.

"Okay, you've been practicing, haven't you? You almost hit me!"

Megan smiled again.

Dexter nodded. "That damn Louie! He's been helping you!"

Megan smiled wider. "Come on, it's almost time for the meeting."

"That's it, isn't it? My best friend has been teaching you what I taught him!"

Megan continued smiling without speaking all the way down to the situation room.

PERCIVAL "KING LOUIE" Washington was the last to arrive at the morning meeting. He had slept badly all night, that is, when he could sleep at all. He kept having nightmares of Donna's last moments, and each time, the knife that she had sprung up and stabbed him with went into his chest instead of his arm. He would wake up every time he had the nightmare, sweat pouring from him...and he'd be stifling the scream that wanted to escape his lips.

Louie blamed himself for not seeing through Donna's masquerade, and blamed himself for all of the people she had killed inside the Justice Security building. But, how could he have known that a glitzy supermodel was really a well-trained Fernandez assassin?

Louie had spoken several times to Dr. Caleb Mitchell, the Justice Security staff psychiatrist. Caleb had often said that Louie was not to be blamed, and that he'd have to learn to forgive himself...that Donna had fooled a lot of people. No one had any idea that she'd been recruited by Fernandez, and her cover was incredible.

Deeply buried training, incredible cover...none of that meant a thing to him, when, late at night, he had to try to sleep. The faces of those Donna had killed paraded through his mind, chasing sleep away from him...the blame and the guilt seemed insurmountable. Then, when sleep finally came to him, the nightmares appeared...and woke him up again.

So, when Louie finally stumbled into the situation room, thunderclouds hovered in his face.

Louie Washington was in a bad mood.

Louie walked to the table filled with pastries and other breakfast items, filled a plate, and poured himself a big cup of coffee. Once he had these things, he walked to the big, round table and sat down. He didn't notice that Marcus was also sitting at the table.

"Good morning, Louie," said Misty gently.

"Mornin'," he replied, speaking around the mouthful of doughnut.

"Hello, Louie," said Marcus.

Louie took another bite before he realized that Marcus had been the one that had spoken. He looked up, wide-eyed, and said, "What the hell *you* doin' here?"

"I see that your hospitality is holding up quite well, Louie," said a voice from one of the room's monitors.

Louie looked up at the monitor. Jessica Queen was scowling at him. He put down his doughnut, shaking his head as he did so. "I'm sorry, Marcus. I haven't been sleeping well lately."

Marcus nodded. "Understood, big guy. I haven't been catching as many zees as I should have been, either. Not since the club."

"Marcus, I believe that makes *all* of us," said Jessica.

"Jessica, how's our client out there?" asked Joey.

"Sleeping it off." Disgust dripped from Jessica's words. "I called her a worthless, spoiled, coked-up, drunken whore last night. She attempted to cry, then took a drink from the whiskey bottle she was holding. She passed out before she was able to swallow." Jessica was *really* pissed. When she got this pissed, a slight Australian accent crept into her speech...a remnant of her father's home country. Jessica was the result of an Australian father and a California mother. "I'm beginning to wonder if this job is worth sparing the time."

Marcus asked, "Aren't you afraid she'll fire you this morning?"

Jessica shook her head. "I promise you she won't remember a word of it."

Joey laughed. "Just remember, Jess – her next big blockbuster movie fee is paying for it."

"Well, bloody *hell*!"

Everyone except Louie laughed at that.

Joey turned to Marcus. "Okay, Marcus, Jessica's transmission is as secure as we can make it. What's the big news?"

Marcus took a breath. "Want another crack at Fernandez?"

Louie slammed his palms on the table. Everyone jumped.

"You damn *straight* I want another crack at Fernandez!" Louie declared loudly. He lifted his big hands for everyone to see. "You wanna know what'll happen to that asshole if I get these hands on him?" No one said anything. "I'm gonna tear him apart, piece by piece!"

Joey nodded sagely. "Marcus, I believe we all share Percy's enthusiasm in this situation."

"He's not in town, is he?" asked Dexter.

Marcus shook his head. "Nope. We got word that he's in Chicago."

"*Chicago?*" said Jessica incredulously. "What's he doing in Chicago?"

"Yeah," added Megan. "I thought he wanted us. Who's he after in Chicago?"

"Not who, but *what*," replied Marcus. "Three street dealers and their supplier were all found dead last night. All were shot three times through the heart, and the supplier was tortured inside his apartment before he was shot."

"How did you link that to Fernandez?" asked Joey.

Marcus smiled. "Fernandez screwed up. There were witnesses that overheard his name." Marcus paused. "Felix Juarez is with him, too."

"Fernandez doesn't take a shit without Felix there to wipe his ass," commented Dexter.

There were chuckles from everyone.

"How did you find out about it, Marcus?" asked Misty.

Marcus consulted his notes. "Through a Narcotics detective...um...Tory Masterson, Detective First Class and a Homicide Lieutenant named Mickey Rooney."

Shared looks went around the table.

"I have to ask," said Megan. "Does he know what he's gotten himself into?"

Marcus smiled. "Not that I know of."

Joey said, "And what tipped *them* off?"

"Apparently, Rooney and his partner, uh," more notes consultation, "...Sam Tanner, were on duty and caught the squeals for all four of the dead guys. Masterson was at the scene of the fourth one when Rooney arrived. Masterson had been undercover with the number four, William Joseph Smith, a.k.a the Tinker, trying to find out who distributed to him."

"Following the ladder up, right?" asked Dexter.

"Looks like it," replied Marcus. "Masterson remembered that Fernandez was Federal, and a Captain Baker notified the Chicago FBI office. They notified me."

"Marcus, is this Rooney any good? Or Masterson? Or Tanner?" asked Joey.

"As far as I can find out, they're some of the best of the Chicago PD," replied Marcus.

Joey leaned back into his chair. "Okay, questions...what is Fernandez up to?"

Always the thinker, Dexter said, "It looks like Fernandez is making a move into Chicago. But, to do that, he has to eliminate some competition."

Joey nodded. "Or make the competition afraid of him."

Misty said, "You know, this could fire off a gang war. Right in the middle of Chicago."

"Say, Joey, could we sneak in? Take Fernandez by surprise?" asked Jessica. "He won't be expecting us in Chicago, and that might give us an advantage."

"That is a very good idea," said Joey.

Everyone turned to Marcus. He gradually became aware of it, and met each person's eyes.

"What?" asked Marcus.

"You have to come with us," said Joey.

"What the hell for?" said Marcus, confused. "It's *your* contract!"

Joey pointed at Marcus. "But *you* are our government liaison. *You* are our grease, Marcus."

"Yeah," said Louie. "You can grease those wheels in Chicago. Lubricate for us, so that we can just sliiiiiide in."

"Oh, my *God*, Louie!" said Jessica.

Louie looked around the table, wide-eyed with innocence. "What'd I say?"

Marcus looked around at everyone, looked down at his notepad, looked at the ceiling, then shook his head. "Okay, I'll go," he said. "What do we all need to do?"

"We'll need a lot of computer equipment, for one thing," said Dexter. He turned to Megan. "Want to come help me organize it?"

"Sure, honey," replied Megan.

As Dexter and Megan stood to leave, Joey said, "Get it ready, Dex, and send it over to the airport. We'll ship equipment and weapons on one of the cargo planes."

Over the monitor, Jessica said, "Joey, why don't you send Charlie Li out here to replace me? Once he arrives, I can catch a flight to Chicago from LAX."

Joey nodded. "Sounds good, Jess. I'll send him out on one of the jets, and you can take that jet to Chicago. Fly safe, and don't forget to let the client know about the change in personnel." He paused. "*Politely*, please."

Jessica smirked. "Stop trying to ruin my fun, Joey." She disconnected the secure transmission from her end.

"Louie, can you get the armament?" asked Joey.

"Sho 'nuff," Louie replied. "What do you think we'll need?"

"I leave it to you, Louie. Picture the worst possible scenario as you pack."

Louie smiled. It scared Marcus a little. "I been lookin' for payback ever since that mess with Donna. Dis'll be fun." He left.

Misty said quietly, "You know he still blames himself for that."

Joey nodded. "So does Jessica."

"They both did the best they could, and there's no way Louie could have known that Donna was what she was," said Marcus.

"Yeah, but that doesn't stop the guilt, Marcus," said Joey.

"What do you want *me* to do, sugarbuns?" asked Misty, wide-eyed.

Marcus snorted into his hand.

Joey gave Marcus a look, then said, "Pick out about ten grunts to bring with us. They have to be the best, and make sure to include Brandon King, Patty Ferguson, and Tony Armstrong. You pick the other seven."

"What about Turk?"

"I'm leaving him in charge here," said Joey.

"Okay." Misty stood, kissed Joey on top of the head, and left the room.

"So, what do you need from me...sugarbuns?" said Marcus, with a straight face.

Returning the seriousness, and raising one eyebrow, Joey replied, "I need you to kiss my ass, Marcus."

Both men burst out laughing.

"Marcus, I want those three cops on the team with us. They know the city, and we don't. But, we also need it to be top secret."

Marcus nodded. "I can do that. I'll keep it quiet. I'll only tell the head of the Chicago office, the mayor, the police chief, and the cops' captain."

"Good. I'd like to have maybe a conference room at the station that this Rooney guy calls home. You'll have to explain to his captain. I'll break it to the three cops."

"Can do. I thought I should tell you, too, that I tried to bring Nicholas Turner in on this one. I thought he could be a big help to us, but, he can't get away. He's working a custody case, and has the new wife and family...I mean, the new wife and kid."

Joey looked at Marcus skeptically. Finally, he said, "We're gonna talk about that one day, you and I. I'd like to know what it is about Nicholas Turner that you aren't telling me."

Marcus chuckled. "Joey, I have a feeling you'll find out one day soon, but it isn't my story to tell. How are we getting to Chicago?"

"We're taking one of the jets. It should carry us all safely. We'll leave about three or so. Also, I'm having one of the stealth choppers flown there. It would be nice if we could park it on the station roof. Will it hold it?"

"I'll find out. Meet you at the airport at three."

Chapter 4

After I finally finished writing all the reports required by the judicial system, I left to try to get some sleep. Notice that I said, "try" to get some sleep. I have chronic insomnia, and that seems to make sleep the big prize you finally win, once you spend enough money at a carnival huckster's stand.

I had sent Sam home a couple of hours earlier.

"You sure you don't want to go with me for breakfast?" he asked as he was leaving. He already had a chocolate jelly-filled doughnut with sprinkles in his hand. I had no idea where he had found it, but he took a huge bite as I answered.

"No, Sam, you go ahead," I replied. "I'll finish up the reports. We're on duty again tonight. Get some sleep."

"Pot calling the kettle black," he replied. "You need sleep, too. See you tonight, Mickey." The rest of the doughnut disappeared into that bottomless cavern as he left my office.

Earlier, I had eyeballed the coffee pot in the squad room, but I had declined to accept any – it looked and smelled as if Saudi Arabia used it as a biological weapon. Instead, I found a desk for Masterson so that he could fill out his reports. When Captain Baker came in, we reported to him what the witnesses had said, and that we were to report it to the Feds.

"Great," Baker said. "More Feds breathing down our necks." To me, he said, "Make sure that you finish your reports before you leave this morning. Once I call the Feds, I don't want to be left alone with nothing while you three are sleeping the day away."

Masterson had finished his reports first, probably because he had only been at the scene of the fourth victim. He came to my office when he finished.

"Mickey, do you still want me here tonight?"

I thought about it. Even though we were handing Fernandez over to the Feds, that didn't mean that we couldn't look into the murders. We could at least gather some evidence and hope that the Feds weren't stupid enough to screw it up.

"Yeah, Tory, come in here tonight," I replied. "I don't see anything to stop us from looking into the murders, do you?"

"No, ma'am, I don't. I'd like to catch this guy before the Feds take over, if we can. That was three months of *my* work that he ruined."

I smiled. Same old Tory. "We'll look into them tonight."

Tory left.

When I finally walked out of the station, I stopped off at the market to buy a few groceries. My poor refrigerator didn't have a current purpose, except to house some green, growing things in a plastic container that had once held cottage cheese.

My plan was to buy a few things, go home, cook something, eat it, and go to bed. Maybe a little food on my stomach, combined with some milk, would give me a good day's sleep.

Right. And dollar bills were going to suddenly be distributed from my posterior.

I did my shopping and drove home. I live very close to "Wrigleyville", within spitting distance of the Cubs' playground. Often, when I worked nights, I found legitimate parking spaces during the day, if the Cubs weren't playing. In early November, the Cubs were out of service until April. I parked almost in front of my building, relieved that I didn't have to use my badge to park in front of a fire hydrant...or the no-parking zone in front of the apartment house's delivery doors.

I left my groceries in the hall as I entered my apartment. I had my gun drawn, ready to use, as I toured my apartment to make no one had decided to take up residence while I had been at work.

The Corn Flakes Killer had done that. Twice. The first time, he shot me in the leg. The second time, he had shot my date, John. John had survived, but I hadn't heard from him in a few days. Comes from working nights for me, and intense physical therapy for him.

My encounter with the Corn Flakes Killer has no place in this tale, but I may pass it along to you some time. Just not now.

So, at thirty-three, my leg was on the mend, but it still hurt if I was upright too long.

I retrieved my groceries and put them away. I left out eggs, cheese, and butter for scrambled eggs.

I called my mom while I cooked. I assured her that I was still alive, and that I would get down to Florida as soon as I could. I wrapped up the call by telling her that I loved her.

My eggs were very good, and the milk went down smoothly. Feeling fueled, I surprised myself. I fell asleep.

WHEN I ARRIVED AT THE station at seven that evening, Captain Baker intercepted me.

"Mickey," he called, trotting down the hall after me.

I stopped walking.

"I need you to go to the conference room. I'll be there in a minute."

"The conference room? What's going on?"

"FBI's here already. I'm going to get Tanner and Masterson. As soon as I round them up, we'll be in there."

"Can I at least drop my purse on my desk?"

Baker shook his head as he began to trot away. "Better not. They stressed moving quickly."

I guess trotting down the hall at walking speed counts as moving quickly. I declined that particular humiliation.

I stopped in the squad room and poured a cup of hot, putrid sewage that the patrol sergeant called coffee.

I entered the conference room. Ten other people were there. The only person that was dressed in a suit approached me.

"Excuse me, ma'am. This meeting is top secret. We're waiting for Captain Baker and Lieutenant Rooney to arrive."

The guy was cute for an FBI agent. His hair didn't have that GI look that so many men in law enforcement felt was the 'chic' way to look. His hair was wavy, and brown, and he was at least six feet tall. He had beautiful blue eyes, and I pegged him at early-to-mid thirties. My heart did a few calisthenics.

"Captain Baker asked me to meet him here," I managed to say, after I had tucked my drooling tongue back into my mouth.

Mr. Right nodded, and pointed to a chair against the wall. It wasn't at the table. Because of his rudeness, I decided that I wasn't going to tell him my name yet. I wanted to see what surprise looked like on that gorgeous face.

The FBI man walked back over to the little group that he had been speaking with when I came into the room. They included a nice-looking, nondescript man with brown hair, a stunningly beautiful woman with auburn hair, green eyes, and a figure that I had always wanted and never had at her age, and the largest black man I had seen in some time. He had muscles that I didn't know existed on a human being, and he looked vaguely familiar.

There were people seated at the table. They included a man with glasses, dark red hair, and a calm demeanor, holding hands with another gorgeous, tough-looking woman. Another attractive woman was seated straight-backed, with shoulder-length blonde hair and had her hands resting on crossed legs.

Against the wall opposite me were three more people. One leaned against the wall with his arms crossed, watching everyone and everything. Black hair, a bit grey at the temples, and muscles said he was military...or, more likely, ex-military. Close to him, seated in chairs next to the military man, were two kids obviously in their early twenties. She was a pretty, freckled blond, and the young man next to her was also blond, with a creamed coffee color to his skin. They were obviously close friends, if not lovers. Mr. Ex-military said something to the two kids, who smiled and replied quietly back to him.

I noticed all of this in glances when I could tear my eyes away from the hunk. I normally don't care for FBI agents, but this one attracted me like no one had. Well, at first, John had that effect...but it hadn't been nearly as strong.

I sat quietly, waiting for Captain Baker to come in and deliver my punchline. I didn't have long to wait.

The conference room door banged open, and Captain Baker walked in, followed closely by Sam and Tory. Tory closed the door.

The FBI man turned toward Captain Baker, who began introductions.

"Chief Moore, this is Detective First Sam Tanner, and Detective First Tory Masterson. You've already met Lieutenant Mickey Rooney," said the captain.

The FBI man shook his head with a slight smile, and said, "No, Captain, I haven't met Lieutenant Rooney yet. The only person that's been here is this lady." He held a hand out to me as he said that. Then, slowly, realization dawned on his face. "Unless this is...," he said with confusion. "Mickey?" he asked incredulously. Finally, the thought formed. "*Michelle!*" he said with finality, as the realization became complete.

Everyone else in the room burst into laughter. The ex-military man across the room held out his hand, and the two kids put cash into his hand. The ex-military man smiled and tipped me a wink. I smiled and winked back. Then I stood, and held my hand out to the poor FBI man. "I'm Lieutenant Mickey Rooney, Mister...?"

Shaking his head at his mistake, the FBI man said, "Moore. Section Chief Marcus Moore, FBI."

I smiled to show that there were no hard feelings. "And who are these people? Are they FBI, too?"

"They are, and they aren't...it's complicated," said Moore. "Let me introduce you all..."

Sam interrupted him. "Hey! I know that guy!" He pointed at the huge black man. "You're King Louie Washington! You won the World Boxing Championship a little while back!"

Now I knew why he looked familiar. "We watched that match! You totaled the champ!" I said.

The guy with the red hair and glasses said, "We can't take you *anywhere*, can we, Louie?"

The others laughed.

"You right," said Washington. "That was me. I got stuck wit' that fight 'cause of my temper. I coulda had the champ in the first round, if I hadn't had to stall for time."

I looked up to Washington. And looked up. And looked up a bit more. He towered above me. I mean, the man was *huge!* "It must have taken a lot to turn down the Championship."

"No, ma'am. If I'd beaten him fair and square, I would have accepted it with pride. But, I couldn't have taken it in good conscience knowin' that I'd deliberately dragged out the fight," said Washington. "My mama back in Alabama, Betty, taught me 'bout a little something called 'integrity."

I looked at the guy with glasses. "You're Dexter Beck, right? You were in Louie's corner at the fight."

"Yes, ma'am, that was me," said Beck. He indicated the woman sitting next to him. "This is my wife, Megan."

I smiled and shook her hand. "A pleasure."

"Nice to meet you," said Megan.

I looked at the woman with the good posture. She held out her hand, and I took it. "Hi, I'm Mickey," I said.

"And I'm Jessica Queen," she replied.

The ex-military man stepped up. "Hello, Lieutenant. My name is Tony Armstrong. I'm mostly in charge of the grunts at Justice Security...or you may know them as the uniformed guards. These two," he pointed at the two kids, "are two of our best grunts. Brandon King and Patty Ferguson."

I smiled and greeted them. Both young adults seemed to be nervous, like children caught playing dress-up.

I asked, "What was the bet?"

Brandon and Patty looked at each other sheepishly, and Tony replied. "So you noticed that, huh? When Marcus sat you down in that chair, I bet these two that you were Mickey Rooney. I won ten bucks."

I laughed, and turned to the good-looking, nondescript man and said, "If he works for Justice Security, you *have* to be..."

He smiled slightly. "Joey Justice, ma'am. A pleasure to meet you." He nodded to the beautiful woman with the auburn hair. "This is my fiancé and partner, Misty Wilhite."

"Very nice to meet you."

"And it's a genuine treat to meet you, Lieutenant," said Wilhite.

Everyone shook hands with Sam, Masterson, and Captain Baker.

"Well, it's nice to meet you all," I said. "Not to be rude, but why are we here?"

Marcus looked at Baker. "Captain?"

Captain Baker took a deep breath, then said, "As of tonight, you are assigned to Section Chief Marcus Moore of the FBI, to perform whatever duties that are assigned to you."

I opened my mouth to protest, but, before I could say anything, the captain continued.

"Sorry, people. This is straight from the Chief of Police and the Mayor himself. Chief Moore assures me that he can have orders issued to you from even higher up, from the governor all the way to the President. You are now under his command, and will do as he directs. And you will not talk about it, under penalty of arrest for violating National Security." He looked at each of us. "It's only for a short while, and you'll continue to draw your salaries from the City of Chicago. That's all I know, and all I can tell you. Good luck." And, with that, Captain Baker turned and left the room.

Sam, Tory, and I looked first at each other, then turned to Marcus Moore. Marcus smiled at us.

"Congratulations," said Marcus. "You've all been drafted."

Chapter 5

While Marcus Moore was drafting the three members of Chicago's Finest, Esteban Fernandez was changing clothes and talking to Felix Juarez.

"When will the men arrive, Felix?"

"They will be arriving all through the night and into tomorrow, *Jefe*," replied Juarez.

Felix Juarez had been a lifelong *amigo* and companion to Fernandez. They had grown up together on the harsh streets of Playa Boca Chica in western Mexico. Juarez had accompanied Fernandez on his rise to the top of the biggest cartel in that country, and had followed Fernandez into the army as the man had bribed and murdered his way to the rank of General. Juarez carried the rank of Colonel.

Only one difference between the two men had kept Juarez from taking the lead in the affairs of the two men, and Juarez was rather proud of this fact.

Esteban Fernandez was insane. Totally, completely, violently *loco*. While Juarez would kill without conscience for business reasons, it was always a last resort, and done quickly. With Fernandez, it was a frenzied pleasure...and, on other occasions, was done slowly, with torture.

Fernandez still listened to Felix. For now. But, Juarez knew that, one day, Fernandez, like the scorpion that insanely stings itself to death, would turn on him. Juarez only hoped that he would have the strength to kill Fernandez on that day. He knew that he should do it now, before things became uncontrollable. He just couldn't do it yet, since Fernandez always came back to some sense of normalcy.

Fernandez straightened his tie, then nodded to Felix. "It is *bueno*, Felix. Soon, we will control this city's drug distribution completely. Our men have places to sleep in the apartments, *si?*"

Juarez nodded. "*Si, Jefe.*"

Fernandez smiled. "Then let us enjoy the night. We must see what this Chicago offers."

The two men walked out of one of the upstairs apartments inside the building that Fernandez had "procured", walked down the stairs, and got into the new beige limousine that waited in the first slot of the parking lot. The old limousine was at the bottom of Lake Michigan...a necessary step taken after the taxi driver had gotten away from them.

They drove away from the building on East Pershing Road and into the night.

JOEY JUSTICE WATCHED the three Chicago police detectives as Marcus made his comment. Their reactions would determine how this meeting would be played.

The tone was set when Detective Tanner said, "Well, I'm hungry. Anybody want to order pizza?"

Everyone laughed.

Marcus said, "Shall we all move to the table?"

Lieutenant Rooney still looked skeptical, but sat with everyone else.

Marcus began the meeting by saying, "Welcome to the Esteban Fernandez Task Force. This assignment, as your captain told you, is way above top secret, and enforced by Homeland Security, and punishable by National Security laws. You will not talk to anyone about anything said or done in the course of your involvement. The highest powers in this nation have chosen to enforce this rule by making those people that disobey disappear without a trace." Marcus paused a moment to let that sink in. "In other words, life and liberty are non-existent for you if you open your mouths. You will find yourself on a permanent vacation in Cuba at Guantanamo, or you may face a more...final...disposition. If you feel that this is more than you're willing to take on, you may leave now. Otherwise, you're stuck until the end of the Chicago part of the assignment. Are we understood?"

All three of the Chicago officers nodded their agreement.

"Do you choose, of your own free will, to stay and help us with this assignment?"

After exchanging glances, all three nodded again.

Marcus nodded his assent. "Thank you, and welcome aboard. Joey will fill you in on what has happened to them since they've met Fernandez, and why the government has granted them a contract to bring this crazy bastard down."

Joey smiled at the three. "Before we start, let's take care of Detective Tanner's request. We have people bringing equipment here from the airport, so I'll tell them to stop and pick up whatever you folks want. Is there any coffee here?"

"Hey, Joe, I saw a pot outside," said Louie. He began to rise to go out.

"Oh, dear God!" exclaimed Mickey. "You seem like nice people. I can't let you drink that boiled arsenic!"

Everyone laughed.

Joey said, "We'll have our people bring coffee, too. While we're waiting, we'll fill you in on why Fernandez hates us, and has bounties on our heads." He took out his cell phone. "Where's the nearest Starbucks?"

THEY TOLD THE CHICAGO detectives everything. From the accidental death of one of the Mexican's main distributors at a limousine service, to the internet phone call, to their failed pre-emptive strike against Fernandez in which Juarez and Fernandez survived, to the wiring of explosives in the downtown arena which could have killed thirty thousand people, including the members of Justice Security. They told them about Mickey Giambini, and why he added money to the bounty Fernandez had put on their heads. They told them about the nightclub *Wham!* and that it was really a Venus flytrap quietly owned by Fernandez designed to trap Joey and Misty. They explained how they finally broke into the club using a tank. They told them about the Fernandez-paid assassin with skills that had penetrated their inner defenses, killing so many of their employees. They told them about the mercenaries that had ambushed them in the city park, and that they were after the bounty from Fernandez.

Then, Marcus told them about the uber-secret contract with the United States Government.

During this time, some people dressed in the two-toned brown uniforms worn by Justice Security uniformed personnel had delivered some equipment.

A *lot* of equipment. And food. And coffee.

"In case you're wondering, we've taken over this conference room for the duration," added Joey. Addressing the uniformed people, he said, "And you guys get *out* of uniform and into plain clothes. If you didn't bring any, buy some, and put it on your expense report so that it can be turned in to Accounting."

Masterson still looked amazed by something.

"I see a question in Tory's eyes, Joey," said Misty.

"Sure," said Joey, around a mouthful of pizza. "What's your question?"

"You guys have a *tank?*" said Masterson.

Jessica said, "We certainly do. And I can assure you that it *drives* like one."

"Yeah, and it should be parked at the airport," added Louie. "Jessica made us bring it, just in case. She loves it soooo much!"

Jessica threw a balled-up napkin at Louie.

"And we have a stealth helicopter coming. It should be parking itself on your roof in about fifteen minutes," said Dexter.

"We've also brought lots of things that go, 'Boom,'" added Megan, with a smile.

"We mean to catch Fernandez this time," said Misty.

"And, this time, he doesn't know we're here," said Joey, with a scary smile.

Chapter 6

I listened politely to everything they said, chowed down on their pizza, and drank the coffee they brought from Starbucks. I nodded at the right places, and made the proper noises at the proper places. Finally, I couldn't stand it any longer.

"Okay, Joey, so he doesn't know you're here," I said. "So what?" I indicated Sam and Tory. "What *exactly* do you need us for?"

Marcus began spluttering, "Now, wait just a minute..."

I felt my hackles rising. Good looking or not, I don't back down from an FBI man.

Joey put a calming hand on his friend's arm. "Look, Mickey, quite frankly, you three know the city better than we do. And Tory is from Narcotics. He can find out things we need to know about drugs and criminal hierarchy, while you and Sam can help us analyze the killings, anticipate where Fernandez might kill again, and stop him from whatever he has planned." He leaned forward, looking intensely into my eyes. "Don't let the fact that Fernandez is insane fool you in any way about him. He's ruthless, and extremely intelligent. Whatever he has planned for Chicago is well thought out, and contingencies have been anticipated. Add the fact that he's incredibly violent to that mix, and that he kills for fun...that spells big trouble for the city of Chicago." He leaned back. "If we catch him alive, you three can have the bust. Publicly. But...and here's the problem...we have to act fast, because Fernandez will act fast, too. Last night was probably only the opening salvo in an upcoming war."

Marcus spoke up. "And, if we catch him, I promise each of you will receive a bonus, equal to a year's salary. Tax-free."

"So, all we have to do is provide contacts and information?" I asked.

Joey grimaced. "Well...you might have to fire a shot or two."

"And...," said Dexter, "...there won't be any paperwork associated with this mission. Whatever happens does not get documented."

Now I liked the idea of the job.

"And there won't be any 'let me read you your rights' stuff involved, either," said Joey. "That was part of the deal when we took this contract. We get the information we need however we can get it. Money, threats, immunity from prosecution, pain...whatever works," said Joey.

Now I *really* liked the idea of the job.

"So, let me get this straight," said Sam. "What we're doing is trying to help you stop this guy however we can do it...right?"

Joey nodded. "Basically, yeah."

Tory asked, "And we're free to get information out of our snitches any way we feel like it if we think they're holding out on us?"

Louie said, "Hey, if you too squeamish to do it, call me. I take care of it for you."

I looked at Marcus. "And you're good with all of this?"

"What I don't know doesn't hurt any of us," said Marcus. "If something happens outside of my sight, how do I know that it really happened?"

I nodded. "I see."

Sam, Tory, and I exchanged glances. I looked back at Joey.

"We're still in. What do you need?"

Joey smiled. "Thanks, Mickey. First, we need your files on the murders. That includes autopsy reports, any bullets recovered, or any other evidence you might have on these four murders. Tory, I need you to take Louie with you, and find your informants. I need information about Fernandez – where he's staying, any threats made to existing drug distributors, anything like that. Do *not* do anything that will alienate your contacts as future sources. That's what Louie is for. Do you have any idea who's really behind most of the distribution in Chicago?"

"We have an idea, but nothing solid," replied Tory. "They're...elusive, I suppose you'd say."

"They usually are," said Joey. "Try to find out something definite. If we know who's got the biggest slice, we know who Fernandez is after."

Tory nodded. "Will do." He rose to leave, and looked at Louie. "You coming with?"

Louie stood up. And up. I tell you, the man was *huge*. "Let's go, kid...I'm jus' dyin' to get my hands on Fernandez!"

They left.

"What do you want me to do?" asked Sam.

"I want you to help Dexter and Megan install the computer systems, help input all of our information, and help analyze what we have," replied Joey.

Sam nodded, and joined Dexter and Megan.

I spoke up. "I have a question."

"Shoot."

"Our evidence room isn't going to give up anything without a lot of questions...mostly, to cover their own asses. The medical examiner will help us, but his reports will remain with him for the same reasons. How do I talk them into giving up what you're asking for?"

Joey thought for a moment. "You're right, Mickey. And, like with Tory, I don't want to alienate anyone that you'll still be working with in the future." He sat back, and turned to Marcus. "Old buddy, this looks like a job for Super Marcus."

Marcus shook his head. "I'll slap National Security subpoenas on them. I know a friendly U. S. judge here."

"So you'll take care of it?"

"I'll take care of it," said Marcus. "And quickly."

"Great. In that case, Lieutenant Rooney, would you mind escorting Jessica, Misty, and I? We'd like to see where the killings were done."

I rose. "Let's go."

I TOOK THE GROUP DOWNSTAIRS and out to the parking lot at the side of the building. Dirty, slushy snow sat in wet piles around the lot. They had been refreezing since the sun went down.

Joey and Misty huddled together as they trotted along beside me, trying to generate some warmth. Jessica walked briskly beside me, back straight and head held high.

As we slammed my car doors shut, Jessica had chosen to ride shotgun. Joey and Misty remained huddled in the back, talking quietly to each other.

"Jessica?"

"Yes, Mickey?"

"What can you tell me about Marcus Moore?" I asked quietly.

Jessica smiled slightly at me. "Are you interested?"

I smiled back. "Oh, no. I have a huge list of men lining up to date me." I glanced at her. I shook my head in resignation. "Is he single?"

"Very much so."

"Think I'd have a chance if I asked him to dinner?"

"You'll have to try it and see. But, there *is* one thing..."

"What's that?"

Jessica smiled at me as she replied, "He may beat you to it."

I drove for a minute. "So, he's a wolf?"

Jessica shook her head. "Not at all. He's just attracted to strong, intelligent women. Unless, of course, he's been drinking. He has been known to pick up some questionable women when he's been celebrating."

I detected a sense of humor lurking beneath Jessica's exterior. "You're strong. You're intelligent. Has he ever asked you out?"

Jessica's smile broadened. "No, he hasn't."

"Okay, so what's the smile about?"

Jessica's head twitched as she smiled. "I think that you should find out about him for yourself, Mickey. I'm not Marcus's dating service."

I couldn't help but laugh. "You're right, Jessica. I'm acting like a kid in high school, aren't I? Mooning over the star quarterback?"

"Hey, what's so funny up there?" asked Joey.

I looked at Joey in the rear view mirror and said, "You just go back to canoodling and mind your own business!"

We drove in silence for a few blocks.

Jessica asked, "Did you *really* just say 'canoodling'?"

THE FIRST THREE CRIME scenes had yielded no new clues. Joey had studied them all, spending extra time at the Sanders scene, lining up the spots with where the witnesses were hiding to check the line of sight.

The last stop was the Tinker's apartment.

The yellow 'crime scene' tape was loose, and the door was slightly ajar.

I was leading the way, and I stopped as soon as I saw it. I held an arm out to hold the others away. When I drew my weapon and turned to tell the others to keep back while I checked it out, they had drawn their own weapons, and were fanning out with a plan of their own.

Joey moved across the hall opposite the door. Each of the ladies occupied the left and right sides of the door. The plan looked obvious: Joey was going to kick in the door, and the ladies would move in from either side to offer cover.

Well, I wasn't having any of it. I was the cop here.

"Hsst! Stop it! Joey!" I hissed quietly.

"Hush!" he hissed back.

"You're not a cop!"

"I'm an officially deputized Federal Agent!"

"I don't care! This is my town!"

"And this is my contract!"

With that, the door to the apartment exploded out into the hallway, and knocked both Joey and I into the wall.

I don't remember much after that.

Chapter 7

The explosion was powerful enough to knock both Misty and Jessica down *and* across the hall. Both women were stunned by the blast, but they had held on to their weapons.

Groggy, and deafened by the blast, Misty made it to her feet first. She saw Jessica stand. Along the hallway, people had opened their doors to see what had happened, saw the smoke from the blast and two women holding guns, and ducked back into their apartments and slammed their doors.

The women had not been cut by debris coming from the destroyed apartment, but the blast's concussion had bruised both in several places. Using Justice Security's private sign language, they assured each other that they were okay. They put away their weapons and turned to check on Joey and Mickey.

Joey and Lieutenant Rooney weren't visible.

Misty, in a panic, moved over to the oddly intact apartment door and flung it aside.

Sirens were wailing in the distance, but neither woman could hear them.

Joey was lying on the hallway floor, eyes open, slowly shaking his head. Mickey was unconscious.

Misty helped Joey sit up. She leaned him gently against the wall as she began checking him for wounds or broken bones. Apart from a big bump on the left side of his forehead and a bruised left arm, Joey was okay.

Jessica was checking over Mickey when the two uniformed police officers came running down the hall, guns drawn.

"Hands up! Now!" shouted one of the cops, aiming his weapon in their general direction.

"Officer, I can barely hear you," said Jessica. "The explosion has deafened and injured us all." She pointed to Mickey. "This is Lieutenant Mickey Rooney. She's been knocked unconscious. We need paramedics right away."

One of the two officers was Petrie, who had enjoyed performing Mickey's joke on the taxi dispatcher.

"It's okay, Tom," he said to his partner. "Call for the paramedics." To Jessica, he said, "What happened?"

"We had come to take a look at the crime scene. The tape was off, and the door was slightly ajar. My partner," she pointed at Joey, "and Lieutenant Rooney were about to go inside to investigate. Something inside the apartment exploded, and the door flew out and hit both of them."

Misty was talking to Joey. "Joey. Can you hear me? Nod if you hear me."

Joey nodded, then winced. "Ow!"

Misty relaxed slightly. "Okay, Jessica, he's okay, and my hearing is slowly coming back."

Jessica nodded. "Mine, too."

Petrie's partner was looking inside the apartment from the doorway. "Ho-lee shit!" He turned to look at the four people on the floor. "And you guys survived that?"

Jessica indicated Mickey. "That remains to be seen right now."

Mickey moaned. Jessica immediately turned her attention to the woman.

"Easy, Michelle. I don't believe you've got any broken bones, but let's take it cautiously," said Jessica.

Mickey lifted her hand to her head. "Owww! Call me Mickey, please. What hit me, a truck?"

Jessica smiled. "No, an apartment door."

"Did you get the number off that door? I need to write them a ticket," said Mickey. She began to push herself up from the floor to a sitting position. Both Jessica and Petrie took an arm, and helped her sit up. "I remember an explosion...Joey!" Mickey sat up straight, looking for Joey.

Jessica held Mickey's arms. "It's okay, Mickey. Joey's fine. He's sitting right there, see?" Jessica pointed.

Mickey visibly relaxed. "Wow." She looked up at Jessica. "It's a miracle that none of us were hurt."

"In my opinion, you and Joey would have been hurt much worse if you had been inside the apartment. Thank God you were arguing with each other!" said Jessica.

Mickey shook her head and laughed. "He's one stubborn s. o. b., isn't he?"

"You have no idea!"

Misty was gently brushing Joey off. Finally, she helped him stand up. He leaned back against the wall.

"Whooo!" said Joey. "What a ride! I don't think I want to do it again, though." He fumbled his cell phone from his pocket. "I have to call Marcus. We need some lab people here, quick."

"Excuse me," said Officer Petrie. "I need all of your names, please. I have to fill out a report."

Mickey pointed and said each name. "Joey Justice, Misty Wilhite, Jessica Queen."

Petrie's partner said, "Joey *Justice?* As in Justice Security? In *Chicago?*"

Joey waved a forefinger at Petrie. "There won't be any reports, officer. We're working with a Federal Task Force, and it's National Security."

"Oh, yeah," said Mickey. "That." She looked at Petrie. "What he said."

"Yes, ma'am," said Petrie.

Joey had reached Marcus. "Marcus, we need your lab boys at the Tinker's apartment as fast as you can get them here. There's been an explosion."

"Good God, Joey! What did you blow up now?" said Marcus.

Joey shook his head. "Nothing that I did this time, Marcus. I was just standing in the hall." He began explaining what happened.

Misty came over to Mickey and said, "I'm sorry. We should have explained to you. Things tend to blow up around Joey. It's always accidental, but he does attract exploding things like steel to a magnet."

"Now you tell me," replied Mickey.

Petrie's partner pulled out his cell phone, and said to Petrie, "I'm going to call in, and call off the backup."

Petrie nodded, and his partner walked down the hall to make his call.

"Okay, Joey, I'll get every available man at the Chicago office on that apartment. What are we looking for?" asked Marcus.

"I don't know," replied Joey. "But it was obviously something the Chicago people missed and Fernandez couldn't take with him easily."

"Could be," said Marcus. "Or it could have been done by the people that the Tinker worked for, to hide their involvement."

"Oh, crap," said Joey. "I didn't think of that. Either way, we need this place gone over with a microscope, and people that know how to use one."

"I'm on it," replied Marcus. "Can you sit tight until I get there?"

Joey looked up and saw two paramedics coming down the hall. "Yeah, Marcus, I think we can stay occupied until then."

FELIX JUAREZ DISCONNECTED the call he just received on his cell phone.

Felix did not want to share this news with Esteban. Esteban wasn't going to like it.

Esteban would need to kill someone after this news.

Felix hoped it wouldn't be him. He rested his hand on his gun grip as he turned to Fernandez.

"*Jefe*. I have news. You are not going to like it."

"Felix, nothing could spoil my happiness tonight! We have ladies, we have tequila, and, tomorrow night, we will have a major distribution deal in Chicago. We will have more money, Felix, so how could I be unhappy?"

Felix swallowed. "Joey Justice is here. With Misty Wilhite. And Justice Security. They are working with the FBI and the Chicago *policia*. He knows we are here."

Felix watched Fernandez' eyes widen, and watched as his smile turned into a rictus. The insanity was back, and in full force.

"Owww! Hey!" yelled the woman under Fernandez' arm. "That *hurts!*"

Fernandez turned toward the woman. "Would you like to ride in my limousine? I *insist.*"

The woman was about to tell Fernandez to kiss her smelly rear end, but she felt something hard poke her in the ribs. When she looked down, she saw the gun in his hand, pointed at her.

The woman left with the two men quietly, albeit with no color in her face.

Chapter 8

The paramedics went over all four of us thoroughly. They pronounced that Misty and Jessica would have a few bruises, but that their hearing should return to normal by morning.

Joey and I, on the other hand, were a different story.

Our hearing was already back to normal. The door had actually cushioned us from much of the concussion that hit Misty and Jessica. But, the door had knocked me unconscious, and had hit Joey pretty hard, too.

The paramedics wanted both of us to accompany them to the hospital for observation. We both kept saying "no", but the paramedics didn't seem to hear it. Finally, I had enough.

I took out my badge and said, "We've said several times that we aren't going to the hospital tonight. Ask either of us one more time, and I'll arrest you for obstruction of justice!"

They quietly put their equipment away. They gave us papers to take to our doctors if we decided to go, told us to be aware of dizziness, headaches, blah blah blah...then handed Joey and I papers to sign acknowledging that we had refused hospital treatment. We signed, they gave us copies, and they left with our thanks.

Even though Petrie's partner had called off backup, four more uniformed officers arrived. I had seen all of them before, and told them what had happened.

Jessica quickly took charge of the uniformed men.

"Gentlemen, please go to both apartments next door to this one, on the rest of this floor, and to the apartments above and below us. Ask if there are injuries or structural damage. Assist the residents as needed. Do not, and I emphasize, do *not* arrest anyone for anything you see in their apartment, unless someone is being beaten or otherwise injured. Drugs, gambling, or weapons are not our concern. Injuries are. Understood?"

Murmurs of "yes, ma'am" came from the officers, and they fanned out to do what they had been told.

Not one of them sent a glance my way.

I looked at Jessica. "You do that very well."

"What?"

"Take charge of things, utilize your people well."

Jessica nodded toward Joey. "I learned from the best, Mickey."

Joey and Misty joined us.

"We've been talking," said Misty.

"What did you decide?" I asked.

"Let's wait for Marcus, if you don't mind. I only want to explain it once," said Joey.

I nodded. "You know, I can't remember the last time I was blown up. Come to think of it, I can't remember this time, either."

The others were still chuckling when the troops arrived. Marcus Moore led a pack of FBI agents, including, to my surprise, Agents Carter and Young. They were followed closely by Sam, Tory, Dexter, and Louie.

Much more to my surprise, Marcus Moore came directly to me. He gently cupped my chin and tilted my head to get a better look at my forehead. He winced as he examined it.

"That must hurt," Marcus said, looking into my eyes.

Joey cleared his throat.

I returned the look. "It did. But, not so much now."

Joey cleared his throat a bit louder.

The look Marcus gave me was full of concern. "You have to be more careful."

Joey coughed.

"I will," I said.

Joey coughed again.

Marcus tore his gaze away from me and looked at Joey, who pointed to the lump on the left side of his forehead.

Marcus looked at it, shrugged, and said, "Eh. You'll live."

The look of surprise was huge on Joey's face. Jessica smirked, Dexter and Louie laughed, and even Misty smiled.

"It's okay, honey-bunny." Misty put a playful pout on her face and linked her arm into Joey's.

"Hello, again, Lieutenant," said Agent Young. Or was it Carter?

"We meet again," said Carter. Or was it...well, you know.

"I thought you two were off somewhere playing with Manny," I said. "Or betting on the horses." That was aimed at their incorrect computer profile of the Corn Flakes Killer.

"You know these two?" asked Marcus.

I rolled my eyes at him. "Yep."

"Do we need to talk?"

"Probably," I replied.

Marcus turned to Joey.

"Well?"

"Everything needs to be searched, sifted, and examined," Joey told the FBI men. "We don't know what we're looking for, but somebody didn't want us to see it...or, remember that we saw it. So check everything, get it to your lab, and get back to us at the 22nd District Station. Fast and accurate, please."

Marcus clapped his hands together. "You heard the man. Let's *go!*"

The FBI men scattered.

I saw Officer Petrie down the hall. I waved him over.

"Listen, Petrie," I said. "The FBI is taking over guarding the apartment. You stay here and coordinate what the uniforms are doing, and be the go-fers for these FBI men. If they need anything, you provide it. Understood?"

"Yes, ma'am," said Petrie. Bright boy.

Joey said to our group, "Everyone gather around, please. You too, Marcus."

We all gathered into a semicircle.

"Dexter, where's Megan?"

"I left her back at the District. She's installing the equipment and making sure we have good, secure connections all the way around."

"Good. We're going to need them. Louie, Tory...you guys get anything from your informants?"

Tory shook his head. "Nothing. Not even with the man-mountain glaring over my shoulder."

Louie, with a smile around his eyes, kept a stoic face.

"Okay, let's head back to the conference room. Time for Plan B."

"What's Plan B?" asked Marcus.

"Let's just say, 'The enemy of my enemy is my friend,'" quoted Joey.

"Why does that sound like something I'm not going to like in my town?" I asked.

Joey smiled, and put an arm around my shoulders as we all headed for the stairs. "Mickey, what I have in mind might save Chicago. Trust me."

Oh, crap! I thought.

Chapter 9

When the group was settled inside the conference room, Joey asked Megan, Tony, Brandon, Patty, and the rest to join them.

"Our cover is blown," said Joey. "Fernandez knows we're here."

Cries of "dammit", "crap", and "oh, no" came from everyone.

Finally, Louie said, "How the hell does he know we're here?"

"Think," said Joey. "Louie has been going house-to-house with Tory, lots of uniforms have seen us coming and going, and we got blown up. All of those things are potential leaks, and, Mickey, I'm including the Chicago PD, too. There's bound to be cops that spill information to people like Fernandez. It's almost a guarantee that he knows we're here."

Everyone was quiet for a moment.

Finally, Megan said, "What can we do about it, Joey?"

"We go to Plan B," Joey replied.

"You said that earlier," said Sam, with a mouthful of leftover pizza. "What's plan B?"

"I'll explain in a minute, but I have to talk to Marcus privately for a minute," said Joey.

The two men went to a corner of the room, away from everyone else. Everyone could hear Joey whispering, but no one could make out the words.

At one point, Marcus said, "You have *got* to be kidding! Tell me you're kidding!"

More intense whispering.

Finally, Marcus shook his head and took out his cell phone as he said, "Okay, Joey, if you think it will help. But, don't count on it."

Joey said, as he walked back to the table, "But I *am* counting on it!"

"Give me a few minutes," said Marcus.

"Sure. Dexter, can I talk to you a minute?"

Joey and Dexter walked to one of the two computer setups. They huddled together, then Dexter nodded and sat down at the computer. He started tapping and clicking on the keyboard as Joey walked back to the table.

"Joey," said Misty. "What are you up to?"

"You'll see in just a few minutes, honey," Joey replied.

After a couple of minutes, Marcus disconnected his call and walked back to the table. "Okay, Joey, it's disconnected, and they're leaving now."

Dexter came back to the table. "I got the number, Joey." He put a piece of paper down in front of Joey.

Joey looked at it and smiled. He leaned back in his chair and looked at everyone.

"Okay, since we're fairly sure that Fernandez knows we're here, and we haven't turned up anything on who might be the target, I've asked Marcus to do something for me." Joey pointed to the landline phone on the conference table. "Mickey, can you show me how to work the speakerphone on this antique?"

"Sure." The lieutenant showed Joey the proper buttons to push, then sat back down.

"Thank you." Joey pressed the proper buttons, and everyone heard a dial tone. He quickly punched out some numbers. "Everyone please remain quiet, unless I ask you to say something."

The phone on the other end was ringing. Finally, it was answered. "Yeah?"

Joey said, "Hello. I believe you're the man that once sat in my office and discussed a...*hypothetical* situation regarding a certain woman with a talent. Am I correct?"

Everyone heard the smile in the voice as the other man answered. "Hello, Mr. Justice. How are you?"

"I'm doing okay, Mr. Rizzo. Is Mickey there?"

There was a moment of hesitation before Mr. Rizzo answered. "You sure, Joey? You know about the extra money he put up, don't you?"

"I know. I'm hoping this conversation will erase any...*disagreements* we might have with each other. Hypothetically speaking, of course."

More hesitation. "Okay. Hold on."

There was a moment of silence on the other end, then a voice. "Justice, you son of a bitch, this better be good!"

"Hi, Mickey! How's tricks for the Giambini family right now?"

Surprise crossed several faces across the table as they realized that Joey was speaking with Mickey Giambini, head of one of their city's crime families. Even the Chicago cops had heard of Giambini.

"Let me tell you where you can stick your tricks, you..."

"Mickey, there are ladies present," Joey interrupted.

Pause. "I apologize to the ladies that are listening. What the fu...I mean, why are you calling me, Justice? I want you dead!"

"Why do you want such a terrible thing to happen to me, Mickey?"

"Three reasons, you cocksu...I mean, you bum! One, the tap on my phone! Two, the FBI people that you put in the building you own right across the street from mine! And three, you killed Vincent Lambosa right in front of me in my own office!"

"And you weren't going to kill him yourself?"

"Yeah, but that's *beside* the point! You put the damn FBI across the street from me, and they've got a damn tap on my phone!"

"Mickey, I don't think you should hold Vincent against me. I did what I needed to do, and you know why. I don't hold any grudges against you. What's done is done."

"What about the FBI across the street from my building?"

"If you'll check, they should be leaving right now. I've cancelled their lease and told them to get out."

"Don't jerk me around, Justice."

"Have Rizzo check it, Mickey."

Giambini obviously put his hand over the mouthpiece, but everyone could still hear him. "Rizzo, call Lesko. Justice says he's kicked the FBI out. Have him check it." He uncovered the phone.

"Oh, and Mickey?" said Joey.

"Yeah?"

"There aren't any taps on your phone right now."

Pause. "You gotta be shittin' me."

"No shit. Marcus Moore is sitting right beside me. Tell him, Marcus."

"Joey asked us to cancel the phone taps, Giambini," said Marcus. "So we did."

"It's fu...I mean, it sounds like Christmas," said Giambini. "Hold on." Giambini's hand covered the phone again. Everyone could hear Giambini, but it was muffled. Giambini came back on the line. His voice held amazement. "My people tell me that the Fibbies are leaving." Pause. "I can cancel my part of the bounty on your head, Justice. Is that what you want?"

"That would be helpful, Mickey, thank you. But, I need your help."

"*Here* it comes."

"I need to know the name of the biggest distributor of shit in Chicago, and I need to talk to him fast."

Giambini laughed. "Now, that's a tall request, Justice. Why should I do that?"

"Whoever it is, they're about to have a big problem."

"What do I care about some bum in Chicago?"

"Esteban Fernandez is about to put the squeeze on them, and we can't find out who he's about to squeeze. Even the Chicago PD is stumped."

"You got me on some kind of speakerphone with the Chicago PD, Justice? And the FBI? And you expect me to give you that name?"

"Mickey, I'm going to tell you something that only a handful of people know. I've been given a top secret contract by the government to bring down Fernandez. I've got free rein, Mickey, and Fernandez has got to go. You know it, you know how crazy he is, and you know it's only a matter of time before he comes after you. We've got to show him that we're willing to take him on wherever he is. I'll even ask Marcus to deputize you as a Federal Agent until we bring down Fernandez, if that's what it takes to get your cooperation."

There was a moment of silence on the other end. Finally, Giambini spoke. "You really mean to take him on?"

"Mickey, I'll take him on with everything I've got. Every *penny* I've got, if it takes it. Fernandez has to be stopped, and I've got the okay from our government to stop him. Are you in this with me, or not?"

Pause. "What happens if he gets away from you and comes after me?"

"Then I'll stand side by side with you, and fight him off." Pause. "Mickey, I keep my word, and you know that. You have my word on everything I've told you."

Long pause. "Gimme a number to call you back on," said Giambini.

Joey looked at Mickey – *Lieutenant* Mickey - with his eyebrows raised. She rattled off the number to the district station, and the extension number for the conference room.

"Hey, Justice, that wasn't one of yours. Who was that?" asked Giambini.

Joey smiled and looked at Mickey as he spoke. "That was Lieutenant Mickey Rooney, of the Chicago Violent Crimes Unit. She works out of the 22nd District here."

"She sounds like a good-lookin' lady. *And* she's got a great first name. Too bad she's a cop. I'll call you back in a few minutes. Sit tight."

"I'll be waiting. Thank you," said Joey.

"Hey, I ain't done nuthin' yet. Save the thanks until I have news."

Giambini hung up.

Joey leaned back in his chair, and listened to the silence in the room.

Chapter 10

Tory broke the silence, unless you counted Sam munching on a candy bar. The man was a walking snack food advertisement.

"Do you know what this means for us, Lieutenant?"

"What, Tory?" I replied.

"All those months of trying to find out who the big boss is! With one phone call, this man is going to find out for us!" Tory was grinning widely, and smacked his chair arms with his hands. "Oh, *man!* I can't *wait!* This could be my ticket to becoming Lieutenant, Mickey! Wow!"

Sam smiled as he said, "That's great, kid. I'm real happy for you."

I smiled at Tory's enthusiasm, and said, "Nice plan, Tory, but there's one small problem with it."

Tory gave me a puzzled look. "What?"

I turned to Joey. "You want to tell him?"

Joey nodded at me. "Tory, if we get that name, you can't use it."

"*What?*"

"If Giambini gives us that name, you can't use it for any police investigation. Remember what you agreed to? I'm sorry, but National Security is trumping your Narcotics investigation."

Tory looked at Joey as if he couldn't believe what the man was saying. Then he looked at me. "Is he serious?"

I nodded slowly. "Yes, Tory. He's very serious. We were told that up front, and we all agreed."

"Tory," said Joey. "Things like this happen all the time. In the work we take on, we sometimes have to overlook certain indiscretions in order to accomplish the task." He tilted his head to Marcus. "He didn't want to stop surveillance of Giambini, and he didn't want to stop the tap on Giambini's phones. I don't want to work with Giambini, and I don't want to work with whoever is in charge of drug distribution in Chicago. But I have to stop Fernandez, and I'll do what it takes."

"Tory," I said. "It's the same as what you do for your informants. They've committed crimes, but you overlook them. That way, you keep the flow of information coming. That's what Joey's doing now." I sat as straight as my bruised arm would let me. "And that's what we're going to do."

"Look, man," said Louie. "There ain't nuthin' in this agreement says you can't go after this drug distributor later on. You just can't do it with what you learn durin' this operation."

Tory nodded his understanding.

"Don't mean ya gotta like it, though," finished Louie.

Sam yawned.

"Sleepy?" I asked.

Sam nodded. "You?"

"No, I had a nice nap after I got blown up."

The phone rang.

Everyone was startled.

Joey pressed the buttons, and put the call on speaker.

"22nd District, Justice speaking."

"Okay, Justice, I got news," said Giambini.

"Great," replied Joey.

"The man you're lookin' for is Pietro Garofalo. He owns an apartment building on Halsted. He's got the penthouse. I talked to him, and he says he knows about Fernandez. He says Fernandez called him a couple of weeks ago, and wanted to 'split' the distribution with Garofalo. Garofalo told Fernandez to go fu...uh, he told him to go do somethin' to himself. Two days ago, Fernandez called Garofalo again and told him that he was coming to town with his 'gang', and that it would be war down by the waterfront over control of Chicago's distribution. It's happening tomorrow night. Oh, and Justice?"

"Yeah, Mickey?"

"Garofalo said to tell you that he's sorry he blew up the apartment, and that he was glad you and Rooney didn't get hurt too bad. He said that you would know what he was talking about, and that he was afraid the cops would find out he was behind it. I spoke for you. I told him that nobody would act on it."

I opened my mouth wide, and I'm sure my eyes matched. Sam and Tory looked just as surprised. Joey had been right. There was a snitch somewhere, and I didn't think it was in the FBI.

"Thanks for speaking up, Mickey. I appreciate it," said Joey. "And please thank Mr. Garofalo for me, would you?"

"Hey, thank him yourself. He wants to see you tomorrow morning at nine. He wants you, Marcus Moore, and Mickey Rooney there. He said he'll be glad to take advantage of the partnership thing, if you'll extend it to him."

"We will, Mickey, no problem. Man, I owe you...and so does your country."

"I'll sure take you bums up on that, too, Justice. Our feud is done. You need anything else to stop that bastard Fernandez?"

"Actually, I could use some troops, Mickey. The company's private jet holds thirty people comfortably. I can have it there in three hours or so."

"You got 'em."

"Mickey?"

"Yeah?"

"Can I have Rizzo?"

Giambini laughed. "Rizzo's smiling and nodding, Justice. Yeah, you can have Rizzo. I got another one I'm sendin' you, too, and I want you to put him right out front. Rizzo will tell you which one."

Joey and Giambini hung up. Jessica had moved to one of the computer terminals, presumably to dispatch the plane for the crime boss's men.

Joey had leaned back in his chair.

"So Fernandez really has called his gang to war?" asked Tony.

Joey nodded slowly, lost in thought.

"So, we're going to war against a criminal, and we're doing it side-by-side with other criminals?" I asked.

Joey slowly nodded again.

"The enemy of my enemy is my friend." I shook my head in disbelief.

Joey looked up at me.

"We can't trust any Chicago PD except for you three, can we?" asked Joey.

I shook my head. "No, I can think of at least ten cops that I know for sure are honest cops."

Joey nodded. "Can you have them all here at the precinct tomorrow on short notice?"

"If I have to, yes," I told him. "Sam and Tory probably know more cops that are honest. We can probably gather around twenty."

"Great. Have them all here about four tomorrow...well, today, actually. It's almost one. Marcus, how many suits do you think we can get from the Chicago office?"

"Probably about ten or so," answered Marcus.

Joey looked thoughtful. "Let's see...twenty of us, another twenty uniformed cops, ten FBI agents, plus Giambini's thirty...that's eighty people. We need more."

Megan, who had remained quiet until now, asked, "Joey, how many people do you think we'll need?"

"We'll need enough to overwhelm Fernandez. He won't have more than a hundred or so men. We'll need at least twice that many. Figure fifty people from this guy Garofalo, and that's a hundred thirty. I'd be happy with twenty more people."

No one spoke.

"What kind of people do you need, Joey? Gunmen, or just tough guys?"

"Tough guys. Knockabouts. People that are ready to rumble."

I thought for a moment, looked at the time, and said, "Do any of you shoot pool?"

Chapter 11

I walked into Milt's Pool Hall with Marcus Moore, the Becks, Patty Ferguson, Brandon King, and Louie Washington. I felt like a rock star being escorted by her entourage.

Milt's had good beer priced cheap, and a dinginess that caused young people to stay away in droves. No music ruined the atmosphere in Joe's...all you could hear was the clackety-clack of pool balls and an occasional laugh or swearword. My kind of place. It must have been Louie's kind of place, too, because he smiled as he looked around the room.

The people at the bar noticed us, and conversation quieted as we walked in. We all went to the bar, and a look from Louie guaranteed space for us.

We each ordered beer from the fat bartender. Fourteen bucks, and we all had beers. The sound of conversation grew louder.

Patty and Megan had garnered a couple of wolf whistles from somewhere in the room. I knew it couldn't have been for me. Patty blushed, and Megan strutted a bit, and got a few catcalls. Dexter beamed a smile at his wife.

"Showoff," said Dexter.

I turned toward the twelve pool tables. As usual, all of them were in use. The elderly black man watched one of the tables, waiting for his chance to play. He was talking the situation over with himself. People gave him room.

I spotted Tim at the far corner. He had the last table in the back, against the wall. He was leaning against the corner, watching his opponent line up a shot.

I got my group's attention, and pointed Tim out. We started over. Tim's opponent took his shot and missed. I looked at the layout of the remaining balls on the table.

"Watch this, guys," I said.

Tim lined up the first shot, and didn't miss until he had cleared the table. His opponent, a young hothead that had one too many beers, threw his cue stick down and began puffing out his chest and yelling something about being hustled.

"Uh-oh," I said. I started moving toward the kid, when an arm stopped me. "Let me do this, Mickey," said Louie.

I stepped back and swept my hand out. "He's all yours, big guy."

Louie smiled. Tim saw the smile and nodded slightly. The kid had moved up and was doing a lot of "I'm gonna do this" and "I'm gonna do that" talk.

Tim, very quietly said, "Back off, kid. You lost fair and square."

The remark apparently enraged the kid. He took a step away from Tim and pulled his right fist back to punch Tim.

Louie reached out and caught the kid's fist. The kid tried to move his fist, but his arm wouldn't move at all. He whirled around to see who was holding him. The kid's eyes widened as he looked up into Louie's face.

Louie let go of the kid's fist and deliberately closed his fist over the front of the kid's shirt. Louie's huge bicep flexed, and the kid found himself lifted off of the ground. Louie lifted the kid's face even with his own.

"Kid, I gonna give you some advice. It's for free...no charge. If you don't know when you been beat, you don't need to be playin'. And if you cain't hold your liquor, you don't need to be drinkin'. Now," he said, as he put the kid down on the ground again. "Pay this man what you owe him, and go home. You cain't shoot pool for shit."

Everyone in our group tried to hide our smiles as the kid fumbled in his pocket, drew out some cash, and threw it at Tim. The kid turned to Louie, started to say something, changed his mind, and staggered out into the street.

Tim was picking up the cash from the floor as I walked over to him.

"Hi, Tim. Think you taught that kid anything?" I asked.

"No. But he did," replied Tim, throwing a thumb in Louie's direction.

I laughed. "Timothy Taylor, I'd like you to meet..."

"Percival 'King Louie' Washington," interrupted Tim. He held out a hand to Louie. "The unofficial Heavyweight Champion of the world."

Louie shook Tim's hand. "Naw, man, not me. I gave that up."

"Hence the 'unofficial'. And I recognize Dexter Beck." Tim shook hands with Dexter. "Now, who are these other folks?"

"This is Megan Beck, Dexter's wife," I said.

Tim took her hand and gave her a piercing look. "A warrior at heart, I believe."

Megan smiled. "Everyone at Justice Security calls me 'Rambo.'"

Tim laughed.

"These are the kids, Brandon King and Patty Ferguson."

Tim shook hands with both. He leaned over to Patty and said, "In my younger days, my blond beauty, I would have chased you to the moon and back, just for the chance to win your heart."

"Thank you, sir," replied Patty, as she blushed bright red.

"And, this gentleman is Marcus Moore." I waited until Tim was shaking hands, and added, "He's from the FBI."

I have to give Tim credit. He didn't seem a bit fazed by the fact that he was shaking hands with an FBI agent.

"Mr. Taylor, I have to ask you a question. Privately," said Marcus.

"Let me save you a little time," said Tim. "You're here, or, rather, Justice Security is here. That must mean that Esteban Fernandez is also here, and you've enlisted my friend Mickey to help you stop whatever he's doing."

Marcus looked at me, then looked at Tim. Surprise was plain on all of my group's faces.

"Man, how did you know that?" asked Louie. "All that's supposed to be secret!"

Tim shrugged. "Look where I am. I'm in a bar-slash-pool-hall in Chicago." He rubbed his hand across his bald head. "I hear things, because I'm a man that listens." He reached to the cue rack and chose one. He passed it to Dexter. "Care for a game, Mr. Beck?"

"Dexter, please. And I'd be glad to," replied Dexter.

A couple of shouts of "Hey!" and "He's got a gun!" from the front area of the pool hall drew our attention. The kid that Louie had "discouraged" was walking toward us. Dangling at his right side was what looked like a .38 revolver.

Before I could open my mouth, Dexter had thrown the pool cue as if it were a spear. The cue not only hit the kid, it impaled his right arm. He dropped the gun.

I flashed my shield at the bartender and yelled, "Call 911! Now!" I ran toward the kid, picked up the gun, and placed the kid under arrest. And, by arresting him, I meant that I sat him down in a chair and examined the cue protruding from his bicep on both sides of his arm. It had gone cleanly through the bicep.

I told the kid his rights and told him to stay put. I told Brandon and Patty to guard the kid, and I went over to Dexter.

"What the hell were you doing?" I shouted. "Were you trying to kill him?"

Dexter gave a dorky half-smile and shrugged, as if to say, "So what?"

Marcus touched my arm...my *left* arm, thank God...and said, "Mickey. Dexter put that cue exactly where he meant for it to go. He wasn't trying to kill the kid. He just wanted to stop him."

"You're kidding, right? Nobody's that good!"

Tim nodded. "Yes, they are, Mickey. Believe me."

"Don't let his geekiness fool you. Dexter is our martial arts and exotic weapons instructor back in the city," said Louie. "He could kill you with a sheet of notebook paper."

"My honey-bunny wouldn't kill anything unless he had to," said Megan. She linked her arm through Dexter's. Then, she shrugged. "Me, I would've blown the little bastard away. Twice."

I shook my head as I walked back to the kid. It was one-thirty AM, and the pool hall would be closing at two. The kid still didn't register what had happened to him, and I had to overcome the surrealistic picture of a pool cue impaling his arm.

Most of the patrons had left by the time a couple of uniforms got there. Marcus came over, and began speaking to us.

"Mickey, if you don't mind, I'd like you to not arrest this kid. Instead, I want to put this incident under the umbrella that's covering this case. Let's just let these two officers get an ambulance for the kid, accompany him to the hospital, and make sure that the bill is addressed to the FBI, with my name on it."

I looked at the kid, and was grateful that he was drunk. His impalement didn't hurt much now, but when the doctors began removing it, this kid would be doing some serious jitterbugging.

"Kid, this is your lucky night. All you have to do is *keep your mouth shut!* Understand?" I said.

The kid nodded, eyes glazed over. He was going into shock, although it wasn't from blood loss. His arm wouldn't bleed until the cue was pulled out.

"Okay. Tim, we need you to come back to the District with us. We obviously can't talk here."

"Of course, Mickey."

Chapter 12

When the group arrived back at the 22nd District Station, they all went into the conference room. Mickey, Dexter and Louie filled Joey in on what had happened.

Mickey introduced Tim to Joey.

"Hi, Timothy."

Tim nodded. "Hello, Joey."

"Before I talk to you, Marcus has a speech he needs to make for you."

Marcus gave Timothy the entire "National Security" speech. Timothy nodded his understanding and acceptance.

"What do you need from me, Joey?" asked Tim.

"Let me explain the situation first," said Joey. He explained what Fernandez had done in their city, and what he was trying to do in Chicago. Joey then explained about needing people to beat Fernandez' army.

"So, you're sure that there's going to be an army," said Tim.

"From what we've gathered, yeah, we're sure," said Joey.

"And I take it that you need some rough-and-tumble people to fight hand-to-hand."

Joey nodded.

"And you want me to find them for you."

Again Joey nodded.

"No problem. Where, and what time?"

"Today at four PM, here."

"I'll have them for you."

"Thank you, Tim. You have no idea how much this helps. And we can pay your guys a little money, too, if it helps."

Tim waved a hand. "Nah. These guys'll do it just for fun. I'll see you this afternoon. Thanks again for the save, Louie!"

"Hey, no problem, man," Louie called back.

Tim went over to Mickey. "I look forward to working with you, Mickey."

Mickey smiled back. "I'll see you later, Tim. Thanks."

Timothy Taylor left the conference room.

Joey went to the center of the room. "Could I have everyone's attention, please?"

Everyone in the large room quieted down and turned toward Joey.

"Thanks. Listen, nothing is happening right now, and won't until nine AM today. Let's all go get a little sleep, and come back around eight-thirty. Mickey, will that give us enough time to get to Garofalo's place?

"Yes, if it's on Halsted. No problem."

"Great. Rest time, people. Go."

As everyone began to leave the conference room, Marcus popped up at Mickey's side.

"Mickey," said Marcus. "I'm too wound up to sleep right now. Is there someplace still open that I can grab something to eat?"

"Sure. There's a couple of places. Want addresses?"

Marcus looked into her eyes. "I'd rather you show me. And join me."

Lieutenant Mickey Rooney looked back into Marcus's blue eyes. "Okay."

FELIX JUAREZ SWALLOWED hard to keep his dinner in his stomach.

Juarez was cleaning up the mess left behind by Fernandez.

It had to be cleaned up by morning, and the body dumped into Lake Michigan.

Fernandez had killed the woman slowly by cutting small, one-inch strips from her skin, then pouring rubbing alcohol onto the exposed muscle beneath. The woman's screams were muffled. Fernandez had stuffed a washcloth into her mouth and duct taped it shut. At first, her eyes showed her fear, and they pleaded for Fernandez to stop.

Fernandez paid no attention to what her eyes were saying. He merely played on.

Finally, her eyes had no presence except the pain, and the muffled screams were garbled mutterings. The woman's body was alive, but the woman was effectively gone.

Fernandez slowly punctured her jugular with a ballpoint pen, and watched as her heart pumped her life from her body.

He then changed clothes, showered, and instructed Juarez to clean up the mess.

Before Fernandez had started on the woman, he had said, "While I am...entertaining...this young woman, I will think on something simple, yet effective, that will discourage our enemies from interfering with our plans. Your source said that Justice is working out of the 22nd District?"

"*Si, Jefe.*"

"I will tell you what I decide," said Fernandez. He then disappeared into the room with the woman, and closed the door.

Juarez had successfully kept his dinner down so far...until he picked up a piece of skin from the floor, and realized that it was a nipple.

He made it to the bathroom before he threw up, but it was close. Very close.

Juarez had tried hard to convince Fernandez that he shouldn't try to control Chicago.

"Esteban, we cannot even control the city with Justice Security," he had said. "Chicago is much too large for us to attempt. We control Mexico. Perhaps we should stay there."

"Felix," Fernandez had said quietly. "Are you questioning my decision?"

"No, *jefe*. I am merely offering counsel. It is part of my job."

Fernandez stared at Juarez, then said, "The decision has been made, *mi amigo*. We will leave that city to Joey Justice. We will take Chicago." He waved a hand in dismissal toward Juarez. "You must go, and make the arrangements."

So, Juarez made the arrangements. Five men were brought into Chicago with each trip. A full one hundred and ten trips, and all of the men they had brought would be in place in the apartment building. Supplies, like weapons and the drugs they would begin distributing, had been brought when Juarez and Fernandez had arrived. Fernandez had even purchased this three-story apartment building. The owner had been very eager to sell, and was very happy with the cash that Fernandez offered. When Fernandez purchased it, the building only had three tenants. Two left willingly, but the third tenant had a new home.

Lake Michigan was filling up quickly.

Perhaps too *quickly,* thought Juarez.

"TORY, I'M VERY WORRIED about you and this war tonight," said Mary Masterson. Mary was Tory's wife, and the mother of baby Adam. "I have a bad feeling about it, and I wish you would call in sick."

"Mary," said Tory. "I can't call in sick. I'm part of something big...something that will get me noticed by people high up. I could even get offered a job with the FBI!"

"And you could also get killed!" she yelled, as tears formed in her eyes. "Adam is a year old, Tory! I'd like him to know his father!"

"Mary, it's my *job!* I *have* to do this!"

Adam began crying.

"Now the baby's awake. Mary, I have to get some sleep. I have to be back by eight-thirty. Would you please see to him?"

"Sure. Of course. Pack me off with the baby."

Tory took Mary by the shoulders, then turned her head up with one hand, so that he could look into her eyes.

"Mary. I'll be fine tonight. You know that." He tapped her chest. "You know it in here."

She sniffed as she looked into his eyes.

"Okay, Tory. Now go get some sleep."

Tory kissed her and went to bed.

Mary watched him as he left the room. She walked slowly to Adam's room, and gently picked up the crying child. She took him to the only chair in the room – her grandmother's old wooden rocking chair.

As they rocked, Adam heard his mama cry. In between sobs, Adam heard her pray. Mary continued to pray until dawn.

The toddler couldn't comprehend why his mother was crying. He just knew that he felt safe in her arms, and her murmuring was comforting enough to lull him back to sleep.

"JOEY," ASKED MISTY quietly. "Do you think we did the right thing?"

"About what, Misty?"

"Were we right in taking this contract?"

"We had to. Fernandez wasn't going to let up. He almost had both of us the last time we tangled with him. You know that."

She snuggled closer to him in the hotel bed.

"We'll lose people tomorrow night, Joe."

"I know."

"Losing people doesn't get easier, does it?"

"No, sweet woman. And I hope it never does."

"PLEASE, DEX?" SAID Megan.

"No, honey."

"But I've been such a bad girl."

"No, you haven't. You've been good."

"I've thought bad thoughts." She smiled as she twirled her finger in his hair. "I need a spanking."

"You need sleep."

"Please, Dex?"

THEY SAT ON A BENCH on a sidewalk in an unfamiliar city. A young, pretty blonde with delicate features and a few freckles scattered across her nose, and a young man with a milk chocolate complexion, an earring, and a two-inch fuchsia afro.

These two young people had been friends for a long time, since they had met in their freshman year of high school. Many people, at first glance, assumed that these two were lovers, but they were very close friends, with a devotion to each other that was much more powerful than if they had been just lovers.

These two friends had graduated high school together, signed up at the same college together, and began working for Justice Security together. Both had been offered promotions to plain clothes, and both had felt that they needed a bit more time in uniform first.

But, that was about to change.

"Patty," said Brandon King.

"Uh-huh," said Patty Ferguson.

Brandon took a deep breath. "I talked to Louie today, and told him that I was ready to move to plain clothes."

Patty was silent. "I know. Misty told me today when I accepted the plain clothes promotion."

Both were silent, and just sat looking at the lights of Chicago.

"Think we did the right thing?" asked Brandon.

Patty smiled and said, "I guess we'll find out, won't we?"

"I guess so." Brandon looked around. "You worried about tonight?"

Patty paused, then said, "A little. You?"

Brandon nodded. "This won't be like the nightclub. It'll be one long street fight."

"Yep. I just hope that Dexter has taught us enough about hand-to-hand."

"Me, too."

A few moments of silence followed.

Finally, Brandon said, "You want to go find some gummies with me? I have a huge craving for gummy bears right now."

Patty thought, then nodded slowly. "Gummy bears do sound good. Let's go."

The two friends rose and walked closely together in the November chill, down an unfamiliar sidewalk, in an unfriendly city, on a quest for gummy bears.

JESSICA QUEEN LAY AWAKE in the unfamiliar, yet familiar hotel room.

Ever since the night of the slaughter at the nightclub and the Justice Security building, and the killing of Jeff Ladd by the genetically enhanced bull mastiff at the dog show, Jessica had begun thinking of herself as a jinx.

Ever since she accepted the partnership, people had been dying around her.

As her father would say, Jessica had the mockers on.

She had had many office visits with Dr. Caleb Mitchell, the Justice Security staff psychiatrist. Caleb had assured her that she was *not* a jinx.

"Jeff Ladd's death was his own fault, Jessica, because he didn't follow your orders. And, the night here in the building wasn't your fault. Donna had unbelievable skills, hidden to everyone, and you couldn't have stopped her even if you'd had as much training as she did. Some people would have died, no matter what. And you stopped the threat, and saved Louie. You have absolutely nothing to worry about."

But she did worry. She did beat herself up inside.

Jessica didn't worry so much about Donna. She was smart enough to know that she wasn't a match for a highly skilled assassin...yet.

No, Jessica worried about dogs. Specifically, Jessica worried about the rest of the litter that had produced the bull mastiff. That litter had all had their intelligence genetically enhanced. A side effect in the mastiff that had killed Ladd had been its aggressive, violent behavior. The other dogs from that litter had simply disappeared, according to their owners. The dogs had been there one day, then just vanished the day that the news story had come out in the papers.

Now, Jessica was worried about the coming war with Fernandez. Joey had worked with some shady people before, but not like this. Teaming with Garofalo and Giambini...she agreed with Joey when he had said that the enemy of my enemy is my friend.

But, was he giving away too much in order to win this fight?

SAM TANNER WENT HOME, grabbed a quick sandwich out of the fridge, and changed into his pajamas.

His wife, Patricia, barely woke up enough to kiss her husband good night.

Both slept comfortably, content with each other after so many years of marriage.

TONY ARMSTRONG SLEPT peacefully. He wasn't troubled by what had happened at the nightclub. He had survived, and he had helped others survive.

When he got to his room, Tony had exercised for about half an hour, then drifted off to sleep.

He reminded himself what another sergeant had told him back in the first Gulf war that had gotten him through the conflict.

Make peace with yourself and your maker, fight the good fight, and if it's your time to go, there's not a damn thing you can do about it.

Tony smiled slightly as he dreamed.

LOUIE WOKE UP IN A sweat, stifling a scream.

He sat up in bed for a moment, trying to calm himself. After a couple of deep breaths, the big man balled his fist and slammed it as hard as he could into the mattress.

"Dammit!"

Chapter 13

We sat in a corner booth in an all-night diner on South Canal Street. Marcus had removed his tie and tucked it into his jacket pocket.

When we sat, a waitress appeared, and asked what we'd like to drink. She graciously didn't comment on the lumpy bruise on my forehead, or my disheveled appearance.

"Are you asking what we'd *like* to drink, or what we'll have that's available?" I asked.

Both Marcus and the waitress, whose name tag said, "Kitty", smiled.

I returned the smile, and said, "I'll take water with lemon, please."

Marcus said, "I'll have something stronger. Iced tea for me. With lemon."

"I'll be right back," said Kitty.

Marcus clasped his hands on top of the table. He looked at me and said, "Tell me about you, Mickey."

It was either a little hot in there, or I blushed. I'm not sure which.

"I don't know where to start. I'm better if you ask questions."

He nodded and said, "Okay. Do you enjoy being a cop?"

I opened my mouth to deliver a glib answer, then closed it again. I actually thought about the question. "I like stopping people who have no conscience...no empathy for others. I don't like the politics, I don't like the paperwork, and I don't like making scary enemies."

"You're not talking about Fernandez, are you?"

I shook my head. "No. I'm talking about the Corn Flakes Killer."

Kitty came back with our drinks, and asked what we'd like to order. I ordered bacon and eggs, scrambled. After consulting the menu, Marcus ordered the same. Kitty wrote it down, told us "thank you", and went away.

"What frightened you about the Corn Flakes Killer, Mickey?"

I was quiet, trying to organize my thoughts before I spoke. "He almost killed me, Marcus. More than once. And he would have, if it hadn't been for my ex-partner, Manny Salazar." I shivered. "When it's that close, it stays with you."

"Oh, I understand, believe me. I've seen some hairy things happen in the line of duty. And I've seen the aftermath." He took a sip of tea. "But, you have to find a way to deal with it, or it will eat you alive."

I started playing with a napkin, tearing small pieces from it. "What about you? What made you become an FBI man in the land of the dollar bill?"

He shrugged. "Much like you, I believed in truth, justice, and the American Way. You have to pretend to see the cape fluttering around my shoulders." He put his hands on his hips and thrust his chest out.

I couldn't help but laugh. "Come on. The real story."

He snorted. "Truth is, my best friend, Nicholas Turner, and I graduated college together, with Criminal Justice degrees. My grades were so good that the Bureau came to me, not the other way around. Nicholas could have gone with me, but he chose to become a cop in our city instead. Once I graduated from Quantico, I was assigned back to our home city, too."

"So your best friend is a cop?"

"Not for some time. Nicky...well, it's a long story. Nicky's a private investigator now, and doing very well with it."

"How did you wind up working with Justice Security? I mean, I realize that you're all friends, but has it always been that way?"

Marcus smiled and shook his head. "No, it was very rocky at first. They had just gotten their first government contract – this was wayyyyy back when Jessica was still their executive secretary, and Megan hadn't even started working there – and I was the green agent at the city's Bureau office. So, they gave me what they considered the "fertilizer monitoring job", otherwise known as a shit-watching job...government liaison to Justice Security."

He took a drink of his tea and continued. "I went strutting into their building and began telling them what to do, how to do it, and when they would do it. It was hilarious." Marcus set his tea glass down. "They laughed at me, and did the contract their way, just to prove to me that they knew what they were doing. I've learned a lot from them."

"I'm surprised you're still with them," I said. "They don't seem like the type to play around."

"Don't be fooled, Mickey. They play around a lot, and joke around a lot. They used to play and joke a lot more, but they met Esteban Fernandez." Marcus stared out the diner's window. "Fernandez has taken them to a dark place, and made them face their own mortality." He turned to look at me. "Did you know that they're looking at Fernandez as an 'it's him or us' situation?"

"No. No, I didn't."

Kitty brought our food, and said that she'd be back. I took it as a threat.

We each took bites of our eggs, and both of us were pleasantly surprised. The food was good.

Marcus continued, "Fernandez has blown into their lives twice now, left a lot of people dead, and escaped both times. He's killed not just people that lived and worked beside those six partners every single day, but he's killed a lot of innocent people. He damn near killed thirty thousand at that damn boxing match, just to kill the people at Justice Security. It's become personal for them...and the U. S. Government is now bankrolling the chase for him. And I'm along to offer 'unofficial' assistance." He laughed. "Mickey, you want to know what Louie said in the situation room about me coming to Chicago?"

I smiled. "Sure."

"Louie said, 'You can grease those wheels in Chicago. Lubricate for us, so that we can just sliiiiiide in,'" relayed Marcus.

I burst out laughing.

"I know, right? That's a prime example of what Justice Security used to be like before Fernandez. They never took themselves too seriously. But, now..." He didn't finish the thought, and shook his head with sadness.

We ate in silence for a while. I was still fascinated by the way his eyes shone in the dimly lit diner. And Jessica had been right – he had beaten me to the "asking out" part!

Of course, it could just be two hungry, sleepless people sharing a meal. Probably that was all it was. But, a girl could hope, couldn't she?

We had finished our meals, and Kitty came to collect the dishes. When she arrived, she said, "See those two cops over there?" She was pointing toward the door.

We both looked.

"They paid for your meals. They said that you had been blown up earlier, and they wanted to let you know that they're glad you made it."

Marcus and I waved to the two uniformed patrolmen. I did not know them, but I didn't have to. Word would have circulated, and Marcus and I both knew it.

As soon as they went out the door, I burst into tears. I was overwhelmed by it all – a National Security case, almost getting killed by an explosion, and the feeling that I was losing control of my situation. The generosity shown by those two patrol cops that I didn't know broke the floodgate. I couldn't help myself.

Marcus, proving himself to be the gentleman that I thought him to be, took my left hand in his right, handed me his handkerchief, and didn't speak.

When I finally dried up, Marcus asked, "Mickey, would you like me to take you home?"

I nodded.

The only other thing that I'll say about the rest of that night was that Marcus made me feel wanted, and made me feel alive.

WHEN WE ARRIVED AT the District the next morning at eight-thirty, Jessica glanced at us and smirked.

Sam said to me, "Hey, something's different about you. You using new makeup or something?"

"Shut up, Sam," I said with a smile.

"Okay, folks, it's time," said Joey to the people in the conference room. "The three of us will go see Garofalo and work out a plan of action. Tonight, it's showtime!"

Then all Hell broke loose.

Chapter 14

The windows of the conference room exploded inward, and let the sounds from outside come inside. The sound of automatic weapons fire followed the shattered glass into the room, and bullets left a long, dark thread along the back wall. The weapons fire spread from right to left, all across the front of the building.

Shouts and return fire could be heard. Everyone in the conference room made it to the window in record time, weapons drawn and ready for action.

A black panel van was driving slowly past the District. Through the open side door, a Hispanic man on his knees could be seen, firing what looked like a military 50-caliber machine gun along the front of the building, raking it back and forth. Any cops outside received a few warning shots of their own, and a couple of cops were down. As the van got past the building, it sped up. Cops were scattering to get to their patrol cars to give pursuit, but something suddenly came through the air, seemingly on fire and trailing black smoke, and one of the patrol cars exploded.

"R.P.G.!" shouted Louie. "Across the street, diagonal, to the right!"

In support of Louie's opinion, another patrol car exploded. Cops were ducking behind whatever they could find for cover.

Another R.P.G. flew into the building's parking lot and blew another patrol car up. When it blew up, it blocked the only entrance to the lot, so pursuit from the District was out of the question.

Marcus and Mickey had driven to the building that morning in Mickey's Beetle. Because it was going to be used to drive to Garofalo's apartment, it had been parked on the side street on the side of the building opposite the parking lot. Mickey was muttering prayers under her breath that it hadn't been blown up.

Outside, cops were running across the street to the building where the R.P.G.s had originated, but everyone knew that the perp would be long gone.

Shouts and moans could be heard from inside the building.

"Joey!" called Misty. "We need to help these people!"

Joey nodded. "Right! Okay, Misty, Louie, Tory, and Sam! You help any injured people, and co-ordinate a triage for the paramedics when they arrive. Dex, call the paramedics, then go help out with the triage. Megan, find some of our equipment that goes 'boom', and take Tony, the kids, and the rest of the grunts. Go outside and guard this place in case they come back for another pass!"

Everyone scattered to carry out their orders.

"What happened?" asked Mickey. "Who the hell was that?"

Joey laughed bitterly. "That was a message from Fernandez, warning us to back off. The son of a bitch knows we're here for sure. Marcus! We can assume that our cover is blown. Find Captain Baker, explain to every cop in the District what is going on, then get some construction contractors here to repair the place fast! Put the fear of God into them – we'll give them no longer than a week to get the job done. Go find Baker, explain what's happened. I mean it – explain everything! Mickey and I will go to the meeting – you get there as soon as you can! Dexter has the address!"

"Right!" said Marcus. He left to find Captain Baker.

Joey took Mickey by the arm and said, "Come on! Let's go!"

Mickey pulled back, and strained against Joey's hand. "No, I've got to help..."

"*No*, Mickey! The best way to help these people is for you and me to keep our appointment! Garofalo is waiting, and he's going to be the key to stopping Fernandez! Now, *come on!*"

Mickey allowed herself to be pulled along, to go to a meeting that she didn't want to attend, to organize a fight with a man she hadn't met, with a man she barely knew.

It wasn't shaping up to be a good day for Lieutenant Mickey Rooney.

JOEY HELD TIGHTLY TO my hand as he pulled me through the broken glass, shot-out light fixtures, and wounded cops.

I wanted to stop and help, but Joey was relentless as he pulled me along in his wake.

We passed Captain Baker and Marcus as we were heading out. It looked like the captain was cutting loose on the FBI agent. I wished that we could have stopped to hear what the captain was saying, but Joey still held on tight to me as he made his way to the door.

We saw the first dead cop outside. It was a patrol officer. He was lying face down on the sidewalk, in a spreading pool of blood. His blond hair had a reddish tint now. I couldn't see his face, because the exit wound had removed most of it. He had been shot from behind, and looked like he never knew it was coming. His patrol car was burning beside him in the street.

"Mickey, where are you parked?" Joey asked.

I looked up at him. I guess I must have looked funny, because he repeated the question. I pointed to the street, and Joey headed that way.

On the sidewalk, we passed a second dead cop. I recognized this one. Snyder. He'd been a patrolman with the 22nd for two years.

We passed a second disabled patrol car. It was burning merrily, and a barely human figure was just inside the open driver's door.

I felt numb. I wanted to kill the people responsible for this, but it felt distant and abstract...like it wasn't really a part of me.

"Let me have your keys, Mickey," said Joey. He held out the hand that wasn't holding mine. I noticed that he had led me around to the passenger side of my Beetle.

"I can drive," I said.

Joey shook his head. "No, you can't. Not yet. I'll do it."

I had my keys in my pants pocket. I took them out and gave them to Joey. He fumbled with them, then unlocked and opened the passenger door for me to climb in. I sat, staring straight ahead while Joey went around the car and sat behind the wheel. He looked at me, then reached around me for the seat belt, and buckled me in. He buckled himself in, started the car, and we drove away from the madness.

I came to my senses enough to say, "Turn right at the next light. I'll show you a short cut that will shave some time off of our drive. Get us there quicker."

"Okay."

I was silent for a few moments. "Is that what it's like?"

Joey glanced at me, and then replied, "Yeah, mostly. Fast acts of violence, followed by the aftermath. A period of blaming yourself, then blaming others, until you realize that there wasn't a damn thing you could do about it." He glanced at me again. "I've been where you are right now. I know you've been a cop for years, but that doesn't prepare you for this level of violent insanity. What I need for you to do right now is reach down deep inside yourself, and pull yourself out. I need Lieutenant Michelle Rooney right now, or I may as well stop and buy some Vaseline, and bend over, because if I can't count on you, I'm screwed...and that's a fact, Mickey."

I smiled slightly at the deliberate joke.

"Now, are you with me?"

I looked at the floor for a moment, pulling myself together. I nodded. "I'm with you. But, Joey, at least three cops were killed back there, and I'm having a little trouble dealing with it. Turn left at the light."

He nodded his understanding. "I opened a box sent to us by Fernandez not long after our first encounter. Jessica's first replacement as executive secretary was a sweet lady named Patti Hoehn. Fernandez captured her somewhere outside the arena. The box had her severed head inside." He shuddered. "I sent her out with her camera to try to spot Fernandez with her zoom lens, and snap a picture or two of him." He gulped. "I never saw her alive after that. Fernandez sent back her camera, too...and he had taken pictures of Patti as he tortured her to death. That one took me a while to get over. But, I did get over it, Mickey. Patti knew the risks when she signed on with us. That doesn't mean that we can't mourn, and we can't be angry. We can. We just have to use that grief and that anger as rallying points to focus on bringing down the man responsible." He glanced at me. "So focus. Shut the mourning out of your mind for now. We don't have time. Later, you can take it out and roll around in it and feel guilty about those cops, but death is a continuing threat to a cop...or to someone working in security. They knew it, we know it, so deal with it."

That made me a little angry. "You didn't work with those cops, Joey."

Joey shook his head. "No. I didn't. But I worked with Patti every...single...day. I *know* the anger you're feeling, Jacqueline. Turn it where it belongs – Esteban Fernandez!"

I didn't speak to Joey, except to give him directions, until we got to Garofalo's place.

He was right. Damn it.

Those cops that had been killed were just acquaintances. They weren't close to me, like Sam, or Tory, or Captain Baker.

But they were cops.

What angered me was that this guy was confident enough to attack a police station because...because...

"Joey, why *did* Fernandez attack a police station? Doesn't he know that it will bring every cop in the city down on him?"

Joey laughed. "Mickey, honey, it doesn't matter to him. He knows that he has to be found before every cop in the city comes down on him. And, even if we find out where he is, we still have to catch him. And he's insane. That makes him just not care." He opened his car door, and handed me back my keys. "To answer your question, he probably found out somehow that we were working out of the 22nd. All it took was a quick phone call from a cop on the take, or from a paramedic...hell, it could've been called in on a police frequency for all we know. He attacked to warn us off...to tell us to stay out of it." We got out of the car and walked toward the entrance.

The apartment house had a doorman. A big, muscular, ape-like doorman. In the lobby, there was a man almost identical to the doorman. He eyeballed us closely.

"Whaddaya want?" he asked.

"We're here to see Pietro Garofalo," said Joey.

"Ain't nobody lives here wit' dat name," said the lobby man.

"Look, buster...," I started, but Joey put a hand on my arm.

"Would you mind calling up to the penthouse where Mr. Garofalo doesn't live, and tell him that Joey Justice and Mickey Rooney are here for our appointment, please?"

The gorilla in the suit eyeballed us again, then picked up a phone on the lobby desk. He whispered into it, listened to the response, looked up and said, "There were supposed to be three of you...a guy named Moore is supposed to be witcha."

"Mr. Moore has been detained, but he will be along shortly."

The big goon spoke into the phone again, listened, then hung up. When he turned to us, he said, "Dis way."

As we followed the big man, Joey stumbled over something in the floor, and bumped into the man. The man stopped and said to Joey, "Watcher step."

"Thanks," replied Joey.

Joey turned to me and winked.

The gorilla led us to the elevator, pushed the button, and held the doors until we had climbed on. He reached in, pressed "P" for us, and then let the door close.

Joey pulled his hand from behind him. There was a .45 caliber semiautomatic pistol in his hand.

"Think he'll miss it?" asked Joey. He had picked the gorilla's pocket.

I burst out laughing.

I was still laughing when the elevator reached the penthouse.

Chapter 15

The elevator door opened to two men with machine guns facing us. Joey had tucked the extra gun under his waistband in the small of his back. We stepped out of the elevator, and the doors slid shut behind us.

One of the men said, "Okay, turn around. Assume the position."

I said, "I'll be damned if I will. I'm a cop, and you are *not* taking my weapon."

"And I'm a fully deputized agent of the United States Government. You aren't taking *my* weapon, either," said Joey.

"Oh, yeah?" said the second man. "Wanna bet on it?"

"Sure," said Joey. "I'll bet you twenty bucks each right now, that you won't touch our weapons."

The two men looked at each other, and smiled. "You're on, buddy."

Joey turned to me and winked. I got the idea.

The first man lowered his weapon and started toward Joey. The man reached out a hand to grab Joey's shirt. Joey grabbed the man's wrist, and quickly spun him around, pinning his free hand behind his back.

The second man, watching his friend and Joey, never noticed when I pulled my gun from its holster. I pressed the barrel against the man's temple, then cocked it, and said, "Drop it, pal. Now."

Joey, meanwhile, was lifting his man's hand up toward his shoulder blades. The man grunted.

"Drop yours, too, marblehead," Joey said conversationally.

Both men dropped their guns. Joey lifted the man's hand an inch higher. The man grunted again, but louder.

"I'll have a scream from you, or I'll break it," said Joey. He lifted the man's hand another inch.

"*Fuck* you!" said the man, through clenched teeth.

"I'm not joking, asshole," said Joey. He lifted the man's hand a tiny bit more. This time, the man uttered something like, "Arrghh!", but he didn't scream.

"Mr. Justice," said a voice from another room. "Would you please release my men? I need them."

Joey glanced at the man the voice belonged to. "In the spirit of cooperation." He released the man.

Very angry now, the man whirled to punch Joey, but Joey had been expecting it. Joey dodged the punch, and then drove his fist into the man's Adam's apple, just hard enough to hurt.

I hadn't moved my weapon, and had no intention of doing so.

A man appeared in the doorway of what was apparently the living room. The man was no taller than five-one or five-two. He was very distinguished in his dress and his manner. His skin was lightly olive-toned, and his hair was dark and wavy. He clapped his hands together twice.

"Ralph! Joseph! Stop harassing my guests!"

The short man walked toward them, moving his hands in a "shooing" gesture.

Joey held up a hand. "Please. These gentlemen owe me twenty dollars apiece." He held out a hand to the two men as he turned his head to the short man. "They never touched our weapons, and that was the bet."

The short man looked at the two goons. "Well? Pay the man!"

Each man grudgingly handed Joey a twenty dollar bill. Joey handed me one.

"Hey, the bet was for your weapon, too, Mickey."

I pocketed the twenty.

The short man repeated the "shooing" gesture to the two. "Go to the kitchen! Go on! If they were going to hurt me, they wouldn't have an appointment! Go!"

The two men walked to the kitchen like scolded puppies. The first man, the one that almost had his arm broken by Joey, kept glancing back, staring daggers at Joey with each glance.

I tucked my gun back into its holster.

"Mr. Justice. Lieutenant Rooney. I'm Pietro Garofalo," said the small man, and held out his hand to shake.

Joey took the offered hand. "Thanks for meeting with us. Sorry about the scuffle."

I shook hands with Garofalo. "I appreciate it."

"Think nothing of it. Please. Come into the living room with me," said Garofalo.

We followed him into a very nice, expensively decorated living room. I caught a couple of names on the oil paintings hanging on his walls, and the signatures on them surprised me. Some of those paintings would sell well into six figures. The ceiling was vaulted, and extended up over twelve feet, with two skylights. A crystal chandelier hung from the center, and twinkled in the sunlight that came through the skylights. The furniture was ornate, antique, and comfortable.

The room was as big as my entire apartment.

Garofalo gestured and said, "Please, sit down. May I offer you coffee? I can't pronounce its name, but the beans are ground and brewed in my kitchen, and it's quite delicious. And, I offer ceramic mugs. I believe coffee is best served that way."

Both of us said, "Yes, please."

Garofalo pressed a hidden button, and a man appeared almost instantly. "We'll have coffee, please, Richard. Bring four mugs. We mustn't forget Mr. Moore when he arrives." Richard scurried off to the kitchen to secure the coffee. Probably after Ralph and Joseph had threatened the coffee beans into submission.

"Mr. Justice, you said that Mr. Moore would be delayed. May I inquire as to why he will be delayed?" asked Garofalo.

"The 22nd District had a drive-by shooting just before we left. A Hispanic man was shooting out of the side door of a black van, using a .50-caliber military machine gun. To cover his escape, someone else was across the street with an R.P.G."

"I did not send him, Mr. Justice."

"I know that," replied Joey. "Somehow, word leaked to Fernandez that Justice Security is in town and working out of the 22nd. He ordered the shooting as a warning."

"That is no way to do business. I sincerely hope that no one was hurt?" Garofalo made the statement into a question.

My gay-dar was starting to tingle.

"Three dead officers that we know for sure. Several others were injured."

"May I offer assistance?" Garofalo was asking me.

I actually thought about it, then remembered all of the extra hands at the station. I finally shook my head. "Thank you, Mr. Garofalo. I think it's under control."

The man nodded.

Richard entered the room carrying a silver tray that held four large, white porcelain mugs, a silver pitcher of cream, a silver sugar bowl, silver spoons, and a silver coffee pot. He placed it on the table in front of us, bowed his head slightly, then left the room.

Our host poured coffee. "Do either of you take cream?"

We both said no.

Garofalo smiled, as if we made a good choice.

We each took a mug. I took a sip, and I thought my taste buds were lying to me about how good that coffee tasted. It was wonderful! I glanced at Joey to see his response, and he was as surprised as I was.

"This coffee is wonderful!" I said. "Thank you."

"You are most welcome," replied Garofalo. He turned his head to Joey. "Mr. Giambini said that you were a man of your word, and that no...inconveniences...would come to me if I assisted you. I assume that extends to the fine officers of the Chicago Police Department?"

With a smile, Joey said, "You mean the ones that aren't on your payroll?"

Garofalo smiled and nodded his head once, as if acknowledging the fact.

"Let's ask Lieutenant Rooney," replied Joey.

I replied, "No one will use anything against you that we discover during this operation. After Fernandez is stopped, we'll begin pursuing you again."

Garofalo nodded. "That is quite...sporting. Then it's agreed." He sipped more coffee. "By the way, I wish to apologize in person for the explosion at the Tinker's apartment. I had no idea that anyone would be back to go inside that quickly. I certainly meant no harm to anyone. The Tinker had left certain...embarrassing evidence hidden somewhere inside the apartment, and we couldn't locate it. We knew that the police hadn't found it, so it had to be inside. I merely wanted to make certain that it never surfaced. I'm so sorry for the inconvenience to both of you, and to your lady friends, Mr. Justice."

"If you couldn't find it, and the police didn't find it, are you certain that Fernandez didn't find it?" I asked.

Garofalo took several sips of coffee before he answered. "No, Lieutenant Rooney, I'm not certain. I'm not certain at all." He leaned forward and placed his mug on the tray. "May I confide in you two?"

"Of course, sir," replied Joey.

I nodded my assent.

"The Tinker had some photographs that depict me in some...indiscreet, shall we say...situations. It was to ensure that nothing ever happened to him."

I snapped my fingers and pointed at him. "You're gay, aren't you?"

I saw anger flare in his eyes for a moment, then fade. "Yes," he replied.

"That explains it all! Joey, if it ever came out that Garofalo was gay...," I started.

"He'd never have a moment's peace from other criminals. They'd be trying to kill him constantly, just because they're so homophobic."

"And nobody would respect him after that," I added.

Garofalo sighed. "You are, unfortunately, correct. I would be dead within a week."

"And if Fernandez has those photos...," I said.

"He will not hesitate to make them public," said Garofalo.

"Has Fernandez mentioned them to you?" asked Joey.

"No. He hasn't."

"Then I don't think he has them."

Garofalo looked curious. "What makes you say that, Mr. Justice?"

"He would have already used them on you."

Garofalo nodded. "You may be correct."

"And the damage in the apartment, after the explosion, would have ruined the photos. I don't think you have anything to worry about, Mr. Garofalo," said Joey.

"Mr. Garofalo," I said. "Would you tell us about what happened with you and Fernandez?"

It was at that point we could hear the sound of a scuffle in the entryway, and then a loud *smack!* Suddenly, Ralph...or maybe Joseph...flew through the door in midair and landed on his back, out cold.

"Mother*fucker*! What the *fuck* you doin' pointin' a damn gun at *me*? *Huh?*"

Joey rolled his eyes at me and said, "Louie's here."

Then a machine gun flew through the air, and landed on the floor beside Joseph...or was it Ralph?

Louie came through the door, followed by Marcus. Louie had Ralph...or maybe Joseph...in a headlock under one arm. He was dragging the man along the floor, and was pounding on the man's head and face with his free hand.

"Joey! These sorry [*whack*] motherfuckers [*whack*] pulled damn [*whack*] machine guns [*whack*] on me and [*whack*] Marcus, man! [*whack*] I thought [*whack*] Giambini fixed it [*whack*] so we was welcome [*whack*] here!" shouted Louie.

"Uh, Louie, I think the man's unconscious," I said quietly.

Louie whacked the man in the head one more time, looked at him, and said, "Hmp...so he is, Mickey. Thanks." He opened his arm and dropped Joseph...or Ralph.

Garofalo looked at Louie, shocked. "Look...look what you've done to my men!"

Louie looked at the two men. "Yeah. There's another chubby man in the lobby tried to tell me I wasn't comin' up with Marcus. *He* tried to pull a gun on me, too...but he didn't have one to pull."

Joey raised his hand. "Oops, my bad. I've got it!" He pulled the lobby guard's gun from behind his waistband and laid it on Garofalo's table.

"Hey, Joe, take it with ya when we leave. You can put it back in the guy's holster. He gon' be out for a while," said Louie.

Garofalo looked at the gun on the table, then looked at Joey. First with anger, and then with amazement. "I don't understand. With talents and abilities like these, why haven't you already caught Fernandez?"

Joey shook his head. "Fernandez has the blind luck of a drunk leprechaun."

"Yeah, and he after our Lucky Charms, man," said Louie.

"Louie, why are you here?" asked Joey.

"I was gettin' in the way at the station house, I was frustrated, and I couldn't sit still. I decided that Marcus needed a bodyguard, so I came with," replied Louie.

Marcus had moved up close beside me and squeezed my hand discreetly. Garofalo caught a glimpse of it, and his eyes narrowed. Then he smiled, as if at some private joke.

Marcus held out his hand to Garofalo and said, "Hello. I'm Section Chief Marcus Moore, FBI. And this is Louie Washington."

Richard discreetly entered the room and deposited another mug and silver spoon on the tray, then left, without a glance toward his two unconscious companions.

Garofalo shook hands and said, "My name is Pietro Garofalo, Mr. Moore. It's a pleasure to meet you. Won't you gentlemen sit down and have some coffee?"

Marcus sat next to me. It sent a shiver of pleasure up my spine.

Louie sat next to Joey.

"Listen, man, I wanna apologize. I'm sorry about the swearin'...honest. I'm tryin' to stop, but it keeps slippin' out. And I'm sorry about your men, but they need to learn a few manners," said Louie.

"Yes, I agree. You must realize, however, that, sometimes, a violent front is necessary to prevent some individuals from acting from emotion rather than from reason," said Garofalo.

"Don't work with me. You show me respect, I show you respect. Real simple," replied Louie. "You point a gun at me, and I'm gonna hurtcha."

"I see. Mr. Moore, do you have any news of the drive-by from this morning?"

With a grim set to his face, Marcus said, "Four dead, twenty-three injured." I shook my head.

"Terrible. It's simply madness to do business that way," said Garofalo.

Louie shot Joey a look. Joey nodded slightly. Louie raised his eyebrows and smiled widely.

"Lieutenant, you asked me about my encounters with Fernandez. Shall we continue?"

I nodded once, and said, "Yes, please."

"Two weeks ago, Fernandez called me on my private number. He was very forceful, and told me that I was going to be taking him on as a partner in my...oh, my, I can't believe I'm saying this with policemen present...drug distribution network. Since I was the biggest, he wanted to 'link' his business with mine. I had heard of the man, of course, and his attempts to take over your city. I wanted no part of him. I invited him to perform an impossible act of solitary intercourse, to which he responded that he'd take the whole thing, and described various things that he would do to me, and how he would cheerfully distribute my separate body parts. I disconnected the call, and thought little more about it. After all, this is *Chicago*. I didn't get where I am by listening to the idle threats of a madman, or by giving away what I have gained."

"Those thoughts weren't quite as idle as you thought, were they?" said Marcus.

"They were not. He phoned me again three days ago, and said that he was in Chicago, and that it was war. His men would be in place by this evening."

Garofalo pressed the hidden button again. "I have a string of, oh, shall we call them...escorts? They provide a good source of income for my organization. I don't have a lot of them – good, clean, drug-free escorts are *very* hard to find – but the ones that I do have are quite valuable."

Richard entered the room at that point, carrying a cardboard box about the size of an old-fashioned helmet hair dryer. He put it on the table and left.

"This morning, this box was hand-delivered to my men downstairs. It was carried by a young boy of twelve, who had been approached by a dapper man with gray hair and beard."

"Sounds like Fernandez," said Joey.

"Indeed, I believe that myself." Garofalo tented his fingers in front of his face. "The box contained two things. The first was a letter. The second was..."

"A severed head," finished Joey. "He did that to me. It was the head of our executive secretary, Patti Hoehn."

My stomach dropped, and wanted to empty itself. I fought it down.

"I see." Garofalo's chair had a small table beside it. He reached over to it and picked up a sealed, gallon-sized freezer bag. "This is the letter. As you read it, please note that it addresses you, Mr. Justice, and you, Lieutenant." He passed the letter over to us. We huddled close together and read it.

"Senor Garofalo,

It is unfortunate that we will not be doing business together. The gift I have sent you gave me many hours of pleasure. As I stripped the skin from her body and poured rubbing alcohol on her open wounds, I dreamed of the things that I will do to Joey Justice.

You see, I know that he is here, and that he will align himself with you. And he will bring that attractive Police Lieutenant Rooney with him, and I will be most happy to entertain her as well.

You, however, will not survive the meeting, senor. You will die screaming for mercy, and I will take over your part of Chicago's drug distribution. After that, the city is mine.

Tonight, amigo, you will bring your men to Burnham Park, close to Lakefront Trail no later than ten PM. We will let our men fight the battle that I will win.

Esteban Fernandez"

"Cocky, isn't he?" I said, after a shudder ran through me.

"You have no idea," said Joey. "There it is. Mr. Garofalo, how many men can you provide?"

"Fighting men?"

Joey nodded.

Garofalo looked at the two unconscious men. "Forty-seven. Forty-nine, if those two wake up by tonight."

"I hope you don't mind, but I've asked Mickey Giambini to send us thirty men. They're in the air now, and will be here in time to join us," said Joey. "Thanks to Lieutenant Rooney, we have several other knockabouts joining us from Milt's Pool Hall. Marcus has several agents from the Chicago FBI office that are participating. And, there are twenty of us that will be there, including Marcus, Mickey, her partner Sam, and Detective Tory Masterson. I would bring more of my people, but replacements for the ones killed by the assassin are still in training, and aren't ready."

Garofalo's face brightened with every sentence. "Does that mean we'll be evenly matched?"

"No," replied Marcus. "Captain Baker said to tell you that we could have all the volunteers we want after the shooting this morning. He said that they won't be allowed to show up in uniform."

Garofalo was almost gleeful with his response. "Is there a plan in place?"

Joey nodded. "I have the beginnings of one. Basically, we're going to try to crush Fernandez, and lock his sorry ass up...if we don't kill him first."

"If I see him, he won't be locked up," said Louie. Since it was said with such force, I decided that I didn't want to be around if Louie *did* catch Fernandez.

"What do you require from me, Mr. Justice?" asked Garofalo.

Joey took a deep breath. "We'll leave from the parking lot of the 22nd District. I'll arrange for some buses for transportation to the park. Between now and then, it's a matter of organization." Joey stood. "I guess we need to get back, Mr. Garofalo. Thank you for your help."

Everyone else stood as Garofalo shook hands all around.

"Thank you, gentlemen. I realize that my business is illegal, and that, ordinarily, you would frown upon it. I appreciate the setting aside of our differences until our mutual threat is neutralized," said Garofalo.

Ralph...or maybe Joseph...began stirring as we walked to the elevator. Louie "tripped" over the man's head, knocking him unconscious again.

"Mr. Garofalo, I'm sorry," said Louie. "I didn't mean to leave my toys laying out in the livin' room. You be careful now, you hear? A man could hurt hisself."

On the way down in the elevator, I asked, "Does anyone trust him?"

"No."

"Nope."

"Not as far as I can throw him."

I nodded once. "Good. At least we're all agreed."

Chapter 16

When the group arrived back at the District, much of the emergency equipment was gone.

The reporters were not.

Joey counted at least four news vans parked along the sidewalks, and each van had their own news crew, all on the sidewalk in front of the windowless building. Each was recording their reports.

"Aw, shit," said Joey. "Mickey, is there another way in?"

"Yes," replied Mickey. "Park along the side street, as close to where I was parked before as you can get."

As he turned down the side street, Joey said, "It's one thing to have rumors that I'm here, but it's another thing completely for our faces to show up on some noontime news show to confirm it." He parked the car, and all four of them got out.

"Follow me, boys," said Mickey.

The lieutenant led the way to a utility door partially hidden behind a small wall. She chose a key on her key ring, and unlocked the door. The group entered the building, with Louie bringing up the rear.

Inside, work crews were busily replacing shot-out light fixtures, and custodians were sweeping up the debris that was left. Some of the cops inside the building were sporting bandages on various places on their bodies. Injuries were mostly cuts from flying glass or bumps from falling light fixtures.

Marcus had said that the fourth cop had been killed when a light fixture fell directly on his head. He didn't know the cop's name.

As the four turned from one hallway to the one leading to the conference room, they were surprised to find Misty and Sam waiting for them. They stopped walking.

After Joey hugged Misty, Sam said, "You people are the damnedest I've ever seen."

Joey looked puzzled. "Why do you say that, Sam?"

"Because you swore everyone to secrecy, and threatened us all with cries of 'National Security', then you let *this* happen!" said Sam, gesturing toward the conference room.

"What are you talking about, Sam?" asked Mickey.

Joey looked into Misty's eyes. "Yeah, Misty, what's he talking about?"

Misty looked at a spot on Joey's shirt, just below his chin. "We have visitors, Joey. They want to help."

"Why would I turn down help, Misty?" said Joey. "I can't think of many people that couldn't help us right now."

Misty smiled into Joey's eyes. "Good. Come with me. They're waiting for you."

Misty led the way with Joey into the conference room, followed by Mickey and Sam. Marcus and Louie brought up the rear.

"Dexter! What do you mean that I can't file a story on your equipment, for God's sake? The people back home would love to hear about this! It'll be the lead story on the five o'clock news today – 'Justice Security takes on Chicago! The story at five, with Miriam Apple!"

The woman that was haranguing Dexter had her back to the door, but turned around after she said what she had to say. She and Joey saw each other at the same time.

"Miriam!" said Joey. "Why are you in Chicago? Or, better yet, how did you find out that *we* were in Chicago?"

"Good to see you, too, Joey," said Miriam. She walked over, stood on tiptoe, and pecked Joey on the cheek.

"Miriam, answer my question."

Miriam waved a hand, dismissing the question. "A reporter never gives up her sources, Joey. You know that."

"Want to introduce us, Joey?" asked Mickey.

Joey shook his head in disbelief. "Lieutenant Mickey Rooney, this is Miriam Apple. She's a reporter from Channel 7 news back home."

Miriam held her hand out to Mickey, and Mickey shook hands with the reporter. "Nice to meet you, Lieutenant."

"Likewise. Joey, can I talk to you?"

"Sure. Miriam, will you excuse us?"

"Of course."

Mickey and Joey walked a few feet away.

"Okay, why is a reporter here, and why does she have such easy access to you?" said a furious Mickey.

"Miriam is kind of...an 'unofficial' member of Justice Security now."

"*Un*-official?"

Joey nodded.

"Well, why don't we call up the Trib? Or, better yet, let's get those reporters outside to join us?" said Mickey.

"She can be trusted, Mickey."

"She's a reporter, Joey! Reporters cannot be trusted!"

"*She was inside that damned club with me!* Miriam helped save a lot of lives that night, *including mine!* She stays!" Joey stormed out of the room.

"*Ohhhhhh!*" grunted Mickey, using every ounce of frustration. She stormed out of the room.

Everyone in the room stared after the two in stunned silence.

Finally, Miriam asked, "Is it something I said?"

MICKEY CAUGHT UP WITH Joey just outside Captain Baker' office.

"Joey!"

Joey kept walking.

"Joey, please stop!"

Joey came to an abrupt halt.

"Please talk to me, Joey. Why is it so important to have this reporter here?"

Joey closed his eyes and put his head down. Mickey moved closer to him. She saw a lone tear running down his cheek.

"Joey, what is it?"

Sniffing, Joey said, "Michelle, you can't imagine how frustrating it was, and how...impotent I felt. I had to hide inside one of the big speakers inside the club, just to save lives. If I had come out from my hiding place, Fernandez would have ordered everyone killed, instead of just torturing them one by one, to try to drag me out. Misty and the others couldn't get inside to help us...it was me, Brandon, Patty, and Tony still alive inside, but I couldn't do a thing to help. Tony had managed to hide in the ceiling when the club was taken over, and he disguised himself as a guard. He managed to get the kids disguised as guards, and then Miriam. And her cameraman, Steve, is a former Army Ranger. Tony got him to help, too. So, Mickey, here's a reporter, scared shitless, disguised as a bad guy with a machine gun, trying to save a few lives. She killed people that night, and she did it because I couldn't. I owe her, Mickey. I owe her big time, and I always will." Joey wiped the tear away. "That's why she stays. Miriam won't report on anything until I give her the go-ahead, she won't get in your way, and she might be able to help."

Mickey touched Joey's arm. "I'm sorry, Joey."

"Do you have any idea how hard it is to hear people being tortured, and killed, and not be able to do anything about it?"

Mickey shook her head. "No. I've always just seen the aftermath," she replied, thinking of the Corn Flakes Killer.

"It's not something that I recommend. That's why this has become a personal thing for me. I want Fernandez finished. Period. End of story. I don't care if he's dead or locked up for the rest of his life, but I have to stop him." He turned to look Mickey directly in the eye. "And I'm going to."

Mickey met his gaze. "And I'll help you." She sighed. "Now, take me back to the conference room and introduce me properly to your reporter friend."

Joey studied her face, then nodded. They walked back to the conference room together.

"OKAY, SO, WHAT DO I do with this thing?" asked Sam Tanner.

Sam was holding a portable missile launcher. Megan was showing Sam how to operate it.

"First, you put the missile in here, and close it up. You set it on your shoulder, turn it on, and look through the viewfinder," said Megan. "Go ahead, turn it on."

Sam flipped the switch. The launcher powered up with a *beep-beep-beep*, indicating that it was ready.

"Okay, look through the viewfinder," said Megan.

Sam lifted it to his shoulder and put his eye to the viewfinder. Inside the viewfinder, Sam could see various lines with measurements, and a flashing red dot.

"What's the dot for, Megan?" asked Sam.

"Line the dot up in the center of what you want the missile to hit. It will measure the distance. Once it knows what it's supposed to hit, a green box will appear around the dot, and the dot will stop flashing. When that happens, pull the trigger."

"And that's all?"

"That's it. Go ahead and try it."

"You're sure that there's no missile inside, right?"

Megan rolled her eyes. "Sam, you saw me open it up, and you saw the empty compartment. Now, find a target, and squeeze the trigger!"

Sam focused on the viewfinder. As he was waiting for the green box, Louie eased silently behind him, and watched the detective's finger.

Everyone else in the room watched as Louie slipped into place, knowing or guessing what he was about to do.

Sam squeezed the trigger.

At the same moment, Louie clapped his hands together as hard and loud as he could, and yelled, "*BAM!*"

Sam gasped and dropped the missile launcher as if it had burned him. He backed from it quickly, got his feet tangled, then sat down hard on the floor.

The room burst into laughter.

Sam, surprised, looked around the room, first in surprise, then anger, and then, he started laughing, too.

Louie, smiling wide, offered his hand to Sam, who took it. Louie hauled him to his feet and brushed him off.

"I'm sorry, Sam," said Louie. "I just couldn't help it! You shoulda seen your face!"

Sam was shaking his head, still laughing at the joke. "That's okay, buddy. Tell you what, you can make it up to me."

"Sure, man, how?"

"Buy me lunch. That made me hungry!"

Everyone started chuckling again.

Louie said, "Sure. Come on, let's go."

They passed Mickey and Joey coming into the room as they left.

Mickey asked, "Where are you two going?"

"Lunch, Mickey. Want to come along?" said Sam.

Joey said, "That's a good idea." He clapped his hands together to get everyone's attention. "Let's break for lunch! Be back here at one, and we'll start working on our battle plan!"

Chapter 17

When we returned from lunch, we found Joey with a group of people in front of a huge map of the Burnham Park area. The map was being projected on a wall of the conference room.

The group consisted of Captain Baker, Tory, Misty, Tony, Brandon, Patty, Dexter, Miriam, and a man I hadn't met.

Joey saw us, and motioned us over.

"Mickey! Come over here, there's someone you need to meet!"

When I walked over, Joey said, "Lieutenant Mickey Rooney, this is Steve, the cameraman I told you about earlier."

Steve nodded a greeting, and held out his hand. I shook it, and said, "I hear that you used to be a Ranger."

Steve nodded.

With a disgusted tone, Miriam said, "You have to excuse him, Lieutenant. Getting more than a grunt out of him is a major victory. I've tried for years now to get him to talk to me, but he won't say a word. He just...stands there, like a sphinx. It's a good thing that he's a good cameraman, or else I would have..."

I tuned her out. I met Steve's eyes, and nodded my understanding. He didn't talk because she never let him get a word in edgewise. Steve nodded back, with a small smile.

I turned back to Joey. "So, what have I missed?"

Joey shook his head. "I'm not sure. We've been eyeballing the map of the area around Burnham Park, but we can't figure out what the big deal about it is. Why did Fernandez choose that area?"

Captain Baker said, "There's nothing in that immediate area, except Lakeshore Drive, old warehouses, and low-cost apartments."

I studied the map. "That could very well be the reason. If it's a war, there's less chance of harming civilians."

Joey shook his head. "He won't care about civilians. If some die while he's taking over, it probably will make him happy."

From the door, we heard someone clearing his throat loudly. "Excuse me!" said a rough voice.

We turned toward the sound.

A man dressed in an expensive tailored suit was standing with his hands casually to his sides. The man was approximately the same height as Joey, five-ten or so. He had brown hair, with a touch of gray. His face was slightly pinched, and his nose had been broken at some point. He had a warm-looking overcoat draped casually over his arm.

I was envious of the coat.

The man spoke. "I'm looking for a distinctly disgusting individual that allegedly tries to provide security. His name is Joey Justice."

Joey broke into a grin and walked over to the man, who returned his grin. "Rizzo, you old, dried-up rat turd! It's good to see you...it's especially good to see you without having to worry about you trying to kill me."

The two men shook hands. "Likewise, Joey, likewise. I'm really glad you convinced the boss about that. That's one job I didn't want."

Joey motioned to Captain Baker and me. "Lieutenant Mickey Rooney, Captain Baker, this is Mr. Rizzo. Mr. Rizzo is an associate of Mickey Giambini, and he's brought men to help us." We shook hands all around. I couldn't help but wonder if some of the blood on the gangster's hands had rubbed off onto mine.

"How many did you squeeze onto the plane, Rizzo?" asked Joey.

"There's thirty of us. Where you puttin' us up?" replied Rizzo.

"Go see Jessica. She's got all the reservations. Do you need to freshen up, or can you help us out a little?"

"Nah, I'm good. Lemme find out where to send these guys, and I'll be back. I gotta show you which one to put out in front, like the boss said. You should see 'em, Joey. They're all outside, waitin' in the lobby. They look as nervous as a virgin cheerleader in a football locker room!" Rizzo said, as he went to find Jessica.

We watched him walk away. We stood silently for a period of time.

Finally, Joey said, "What?"

"Nothing, Joey," I answered.

He turned toward me. "Come on, Mickey, I know you have something to say."

I looked at him, and kept my face straight as I said, "Nice people you hang out with."

Joey looked like he was trying to be angry, but then he burst out laughing. So did I.

"You're a smartass, you know that, lady?" said Joey.

I just smiled and walked to the computer stations.

I heard Captain Baker say behind me, "See what I have to put up with? I don't know which is worse – her, or this Fernandez guy."

I heard Joey start laughing again.

Megan was sitting beside Dexter as he spoke into a microphone. There was a small camera clipped to the top of the monitor. On the screen, a man was talking furiously to Dexter. All I could see was the man's head. He had Oriental features, black hair, and wore glasses similar to the ones Dexter wore. I could hear what he was saying as I got closer.

"But, Dexter, man, she keeps flirting with me! And she's *sober* when she does that!"

"Look, Charlie, you wanted my advice, and I gave it to you," said Dexter. "I just don't think it would work out between the two of you. Jessica said that her drinking alone was legendary, and, if you add in the drugs, you're biting off way more than you can chew."

Megan told him, "Charlie, Hollywood has gotten to her. She's either going to burn out and wind up in rehab, or O.D. some night. Either way, your heart will be broken. You just don't need to get mixed up with an alcoholic and drug user. It's heartbreak all around."

"Maybe you're right...maybe I should just...hey, who's that behind you?" asked the man on the screen.

Megan had seen me from the corner of her eye. "That's Mickey, Charlie. Get up, Dex, let Mickey sit down!"

Dexter stood and gestured for me to sit. I did.

Megan said, "Charlie Li, this is Lieutenant Michelle 'Mickey' Rooney of the Chicago PD. Mickey, this is Charlie Li, one of our plainclothes people."

I realized now what the camera and microphone were for. It was for communicating face to face using the Internet. I smiled at the man on the screen and said, "Hi. I'm Mickey."

"Hi. I've heard a lot about you, Mickey. I'm Charlie."

"Charlie is in Los Angeles right now. He took over a job from Jessica, so that she could be here."

"Wow," I said.

"He's babysitting a paranoid Oscar-winning actress right now," continued Megan. "He thinks he's falling in love with her, but it wouldn't work out."

"Why wouldn't it work out, Charlie?" I asked.

"She drinks. And she's a user. Megan and Dexter don't think I should get involved with her right now."

"Who's the actress?"

"Carly Stewart."

I whistled. "Wow. The tabloids are full of her! Charlie, I think Megan and Dexter are right. You don't need that kind of woman in your life. She'd crash and burn, and pull you down with her. Someone needs to get her to rehab. If she comes out all dry and drug-free, and still remembers who you are, then, maybe you can have something together. Free advice from the Chicago PD."

Charlie looked dejected, but he sounded hopeful. "Thank you, Mickey."

"You're welcome."

Joey called, "Hey! Can everyone meet me at the map, please?"

Dexter said, "We have to go, Charlie. Hang in there, okay?"

"Will do. Bye, guys."

Dexter disconnected the computer link, and the three of us joined everyone else at the projected map.

Joey had found a yardstick, and was using it as a pointer. He pointed it at Burnham Park.

"This is Burnham Park. This is where Fernandez is having his showdown with Garofalo. We don't know why he's chosen this site, but it actually might work to our advantage." He moved his yardstick. "This is Lake Michigan...more specifically, the 31st Street Harbor. He can't back up much, if Burnham Park is the place he's chosen. Now, we've analyzed the area, and we've found three buildings large enough to hold all of our people. There's an apartment building on East Groveland. The grounds and the parking lot look big enough to hold a lot of people. That's where I'm putting Garofalo and his men. Now on East 33rd Street, there's what looks like the tennis courts and parking lots for an apartment building. Rizzo, that's where I'm putting you and your men. You'll have a group of locals with you, led by a good guy named Timothy Taylor." He looked at Captain Baker. "Captain, I want you and your volunteer cops hiding in the apartment complex here on 33rd *Place*, not Street. We'll all have radios, and we'll coordinate the attack. Once Fernandez has his people inside Burnham Park, Garofalo will move his people out toward the harbor at the same time that Rizzo moves his group. You'll create a skirmish line from the park to the harbor. Once you each have a couple of people in position at the water's edge, Captain Baker will move out with his volunteer cops, and form another front, which, hopefully, will leave Fernandez and his people boxed in with nowhere to go." Joey brought down his yardstick. "They'll either fight or surrender. I hope they surrender, but I don't expect that to happen without a fight. Questions?"

Marcus said, "Where will I be?"

"Good question. My people and the FBI guys will wait for assignments once we see how many people we have. They will be used to even up the number of people at each location. I want Louie, Dexter, Megan, and Sam with Garofalo. I don't trust him. Tony. You, Brandon, and Patty are with Rizzo. Jessica, you are with Captain Baker, and you know what to do. I want three people with me: Misty, Mickey, and Tory. The four of us will help when and where we can, but we'll mainly be looking for Fernandez. I hope I find him. I hope I find him and I hope that I can keep from killing him outright." He looked around the room. "Everyone else will be divided up to even out the numbers. Miriam, you and Steve can stay with my group, but any news stories have to be cleared by Marcus or me. Any other questions?"

No one had any.

"Okay, weapons will be distributed to you at the site. I want them all back, plus any that you capture from any of the Fernandez people. We'll also have Kevlar vests for those that want them, and I'm sure the volunteer police will bring their own. Buses have been arranged, and will be here at five o'clock to pick us up, and deliver us to the site. I'll say this, and I'll stress the point: Give them the chance to surrender. If they won't surrender, and if you have to shoot, shoot to wound, not to kill. Some of these guys that Fernandez will bring won't speak English, and have no idea why they're here. All they will know is that Fernandez has threatened them, or their families, if they didn't agree to do this. *So don't kill unless you absolutely have to!*"

Conversation buzzed at this directive, but no one could offer a reason to ignore it. The objective was to stop a war, not to participate in one if we could help it.

My respect for Joey Justice grew when he gave that order.

"Captain Baker, would you and Rizzo join me for a private conference? Tony, Mickey, Misty...you all had better listen in on this, too."

Chapter 18

Joey gathered all of us around in a far corner of the conference room, under a window. Repairmen had shown up, and had started to put glass back into the windows. They were slightly above our heads, and were outside, so they couldn't hear what was said.

"I've deliberately did the briefing of the plan without Garofalo on purpose. Rizzo, tell these folks what you told me," said Joey.

"I checked in with *my* Mickey. He says that Garofalo is going to kill all of the men that Fernandez brings. Since he's got that immunity thing, he thinks it's a free ticket to do what he wants," said Rizzo. "Hell, even Mickey knows that it only applies to stuff meant to bring down Fernandez, not a bunch of innocent people."

"That little...!" I started to say something, and remembered my promise not to let it be known that Garofalo was gay. At least I was able to keep my word.

"Yeah, I hear you, Mickey. Okay, Captain, your cops need to be in uniform, because I have a plan. We'll coordinate this by radio, but we're letting Garofalo's men get a slight head start on the rest of us. We'll leave them out there long enough to attract the attention of Fernandez' people. Then, we'll move into place. Rizzo, it'll be up to you to hustle up your group. You'll be guarding any Fernandez people that surrender from being killed by Garofalo. Once you've done that, Captain Baker will swoop in and...well...you're welcome to any of Garofalo's people that you want to arrest, but only if they gun down unarmed people."

Captain Baker nodded. "Understood."

"Now, Captain, there's one more thing that you need to know. Jessica is going with your group for a reason," continued Joey. "Fernandez knows we're here, and we think it's because of a leak in your department."

The captain's face grew dark.

"I know, it's hard to find out that you might have been betrayed, but it's what we think. Jessica thinks she knows which cop is working for Fernandez, so her job is to watch that cop, and either bring him in, or bring him down, as the situation warrants. I'm sorry."

"Are you certain that it's a cop?" I asked.

"Mickey, think about last night's explosion. There were two uniforms there at first. What happened?" asked Joey.

I thought about it, and said, "Petrie was there with us..." My eyes widened. "But his partner went down the hall away from us to call off the backup!"

Joey smiled. "Jessica caught it, and it bothered her. So, she told me about it."

"And you think that Petrie's partner is Fernandez' man?"

"We're fairly certain of it."

Captain Baker said, "Why don't we just bring him in and question him?"

"Captain, we can't. We're not sure that it's him. That's why Jessica is going to keep an eye on him," explained Joey. "She wants to catch him feeding information to Fernandez."

"Okay," replied Captain Baker. "Whatever you think is best, Justice. If you don't need me for anything else for a while, I'm going to my office and try to get word to the volunteers to come in uniform."

Captain Baker left the conference room.

"Boss, I need to go brief the kids and the rest of the grunts," said Tony.

"Sure, Tony," replied Joey.

Tony left, and Rizzo went with him.

I looked at Joey. "'Grunts'? I meant to ask earlier what that means."

Misty smiled. "It's the company nickname for the uniformed personnel."

"I know that much...But it's because...?" I asked.

Still smiling, Misty replied, "Because they do all the grunt work, like banks, or stores...anyplace that needs someone that looks like authority. Just like uniformed cops."

I nodded. "Gotcha."

I noticed that Joey was holding Misty's hand tightly. Misty noticed that I noticed, and winked at me.

Marcus came into the room. I had no idea where he had been, but I felt my heart jump when I saw him.

Or maybe it was indigestion.

He came over to us. "Want to meet me at the map?"

We all nodded.

"Great, I'll be there in a minute." Marcus walked over to the computer stations, and conversed with Dexter for a minute.

Dexter listened, then his fingers flew over the keyboard. When he was done, the projected map had changed.

It was a satellite image of the 31st Street Harbor.

When Marcus came back, he said, "Why has Fernandez chosen Burnham Park? It has to be something to do with the harbor. This is a real-time photo, so help me look."

We studied the map.

I said, "How about the boats docked in the harbor? Anything out of the ordinary?"

Marcus shook his head. "No. I've sent Carter and Young down to check them out, but nothing appears suspicious."

Joey pointed to a concrete area. "What's that?"

"That's the skate park," I said. "It's for skateboarders."

We studied the photo a little more.

Finally, Joey shook his head. "I don't get it."

Misty said, "Maybe we don't have to get it. Fernandez *is* insane. Maybe it makes sense to him somehow."

Marcus added, "Maybe he thinks that he can just throw Garofalo's people into the water."

"Maybe he's going to sit on the docks and drink tequila," I said. "There's nothing there!"

"Maybe Mickey has a point," said Joey. "Whatever the reason that Fernandez chose Burnham Park, the only thing that we can do is to pay close attention to the situation. He may throw in a monkey wrench that we didn't think of."

THE BUSES THAT HAD been ordered began arriving at three-fifteen. They parked in a line along the curb, across the street from the station, and left their engines running. They stood like big silver sentinels on guard, growling quietly. Diesel fumes wafted through the area.

When bus number seven arrived, all of the drivers exited their buses. Marcus stepped out into the cold to sign the rental forms, and a couple of company cars came to pick up the drivers.

Workers had all finished installing windows on the building by three-thirty. The work had been completed in record time, because Marcus had told the contractor that there would be a ten grand bonus for them if they got all of the shot-out windows replaced by the end of the day. So, on the outside, the station looked much like it always did, but with a few chipped pieces of masonry.

At three-forty-five, Tim popped into my office. I had escaped there for a few moments of report writing. Believe it or not, I had cases piling up besides Justice Security and Fernandez.

It was also the calm before the night's storm.

"I have to commend you on your makeup. I don't think I've ever seen such a nice blending of black, blue, purple, and sick yellow," said Tim. He gestured toward my forehead.

"You should see my arm. Reminds me of a kaleidoscope I had when I was a kid. Hi, Tim, did you check in with Joey?"

"No, but I'm on my way to him now. I brought forty-seven guys with me. It's all I could scrounge up on short notice."

"Joey will be happy to hear it. I know I am. I'd really like this to end with nobody getting shot, killed, or permanently maimed. If we can overwhelm them with numbers, they might surrender peacefully."

Tim smiled. "That would be nice, wouldn't it?" He stood up. "Where can I find Joey?"

"He's probably still in the conference room." I gave him directions. "If he isn't there, he's out in the parking lot."

"Thanks. See you after?"

"Sure, but I don't know how well I can play. My arm is still a little sore."

Another smile. "Good. Maybe I can win my beer bill." With a small wave, he was gone.

I turned back to the report writing. I didn't get much written before Joey popped in.

"Are you ready, Mickey? We could sure use your help loading these buses and getting them on their way."

I turned off my computer and said, "Let's go."

As we walked out, I couldn't help but think that this would wind up being one more layer on the shit cake.

Chapter 19

The parking lot at the 22nd District Police Station was packed with people. The crowd was calm, considering the mix of police, security personnel, FBI agents, criminals, and just plain people. There were some laughs, lots of conversation, and general camaraderie. Most were dressed warmly, and were moving back and forth on their feet to try to stay warm.

If Joey hadn't been so concerned about the upcoming confrontation with Fernandez, he would have been proud of the fact that so many people were coming together to fight a common enemy.

Joey looked at the crowd and was taken by surprise for a moment, enough to stop in his tracks. He had been counting on a couple of hundred people, but there were at least four hundred in the parking lot, maybe more.

"Holy shit," Joey murmured to Mickey. "I wasn't expecting this many people!"

Mickey pointed down the street. "Look there. Isn't that a line of cars coming this way? I bet that's Garofalo."

A black town car was in the lead, with several dark cars and vans behind it. Joey counted eleven cars and eight vans. The doors on the car immediately behind the town car opened, and four men got out, looked around, and went to the town car. One opened the rear door, and Pietro Garofalo stepped out, along with three other men. Looking like a rock star's entourage, Garofalo and his men crossed the street to Joey and Mickey.

Using a totally different, deeper voice than he had used that morning, Garofalo said, "Justice. Lieutenant. What's the plan?"

With a cryptic smile, Joey said, "I'm so glad you asked, Mr. Garofalo. Can we speak privately?"

"Sure." Garofalo motioned to his men to hang back.

Joey looked at Mickey. "You want to go start divvying everyone up into groups for me? I may be a minute."

Garofalo motioned for his men to follow Mickey.

"What's up, Justice?" asked Garofalo.

"I just wanted to make sure you understand that if any of the Fernandez people want to surrender, they're going to be allowed to do just that."

Garofalo looked slightly surprised. "What are you implying, Justice?"

Joey stared intensely into Garofalo's eyes. "I'm saying that if any stray bullets injure someone that wants to surrender, that a stray bullet can find you just as easily. Might even be likely to." Then he smiled. "*Capisci?*"

Garofalo looked into Joey's eyes, gauging the seriousness in them. He saw what he was looking for, swallowed, then blinked. "Mickey told me that you weren't someone to mess with. I'll do as you ask, Justice. But I won't like it. I won't forget it, either." He turned his back on Joey, and walked toward the parking lot, muttering to himself.

Joey thought that Garofalo wanted a drink, because he heard Garofalo mumble the word "tequila".

Joey shook his head and followed the criminal to the parking lot, thinking to himself. *What* is *it with guys like Garofalo and Giambini? Don't they realize how transparent they can be?*

I TRIED TO CATCH EVERYONE'S attention, but not a lot of people were paying attention. The boisterous laughter mixed in with the outrageous bravado so loudly that I doubt I could have been heard over the noise, even if I shouted.

Then I saw Garofalo enter the parking lot and stand next to his men. Joey followed, and saw the problem that I was having. He nodded to me, then walked over to some of the cops. They pointed to a patrol car. Joey shook hands with a couple of them, and went over to the car. He opened the door, leaned in, and came out with a megaphone. He held it in the air, smiling, and waved it at me.

I grinned in spite of myself.

Joey made his way over to me, and grabbed Louie along the way.

When they got to me, Joey said, "Try this. This part is your show. Now, relax."

As soon as he said 'relax', Louie surprised me by picking me by the waist and lifting me into the air. He set me down gently on the hood of a patrol car.

"That'll help, Mickey," said Louie.

I grinned down at him, and mouthed, "Thank you."

I turned the megaphone on. It gave off a feedback whine, then settled down.

"Could I have your attention, please? Hello? Hey!"

Everyone turned their heads toward me.

"Thank you! For those of you that don't know me, I'm Lieutenant Mickey Rooney of the Violent Crimes Unit. We're gathered today to stop a threat to National Security, and his name is Esteban Fernandez. You've all heard of the things he's done in another city, so I don't have to explain. He and his men will be at Burnham Park this evening, and we're going to stop him!" There were lots of cheers and applause. I pointed to Joey. "This is Joey Justice. He's in charge of this whole affair, with the assistance of the FBI. I assume you've heard of him, too." More cheers and applause. "Before we go any further, Joey will say a few words to you." Cheers and applause as Joey climbed on to the hood of the patrol car, and took the megaphone from me with a smile.

"Hi, guys!" said Joey. Shouts of "hi" and cheers followed. "Thanks for coming to help us stop this madman." They cheered more. "Listen: this is a top secret operation today, so don't talk about it after today." Groans and cries of "awww, man" floated around the parking lot. "I'm sorry, but that's the way it is. If you talk about it after today, that man," he pointed at Marcus, "will come and take you away to a place that is so secret, it doesn't even have a name." Mostly silence. "Esteban Fernandez has called his gang to war to try to take over the drug distribution of the city of Chicago. This isn't just a threat to those that distribute drugs in this fair city. It's a threat to every citizen in Chicago!" Boos and catcalls. "You've seen the violence perpetrated by the Fernandez cartel in Mexico, and the violence he's done in the United States. But we will not allow that to happen tonight!" Cheers and applause. "Tonight, we stop a madman, and put an end to his threats!" More cheers and applause. "I've been authorized by the Federal government to compensate each of you for tonight's efforts. You'll each receive a thousand dollars personally, tax-free, for assisting us!" Loud cheers. "And, if the worst should happen and one of you is killed or severely injured, you and your families will be taken care of for as long as needed. On that, you have my word!" More cheers, but not quite as enthusiastic, as the gathered individuals reflected on the fact that they may not survive the evening. "Now, I'm giving the spotlight back to Mickey Rooney. She's a lot prettier than I am, anyway."

Joey turned and gave me the megaphone as the crowd cheered. I leaned over and whispered in his ear, "Garofalo may think you're prettier than I am."

Joey made a face at me, and climbed off of the car hood.

I started speaking into the megaphone.

"We're going to separate off into groups and load into the buses now. Pay close attention, because it's going to be close quarters. The buses may be standing room only."

Groans came from the crowd.

I told everyone that equipment vans would be following them as unobtrusively as possible. They would be given vests and weapons on site, and selected leaders would have encrypted radios.

"These radios are encrypted for a reason, so maintain silence on your normal radios. We never know who might be listening."

While I was dividing up the troops, Joey pulled the leaders away into a group of their own. I guessed that he was laying out his plan to box Fernandez in, and overwhelm his men with numbers. This was the first time that Garofalo had heard the plan, so I sort of watched him as Joey laid it out.

Garofalo showed no emotion, only nodding his understanding and agreement.

Finally, the troops were divided up into the buses. I had been correct – it was standing room only on all seven buses. Joey had secured several U-Haul box trucks to carry the equipment to the different staging areas, and the parade was leaving at five o'clock.

Joey was finishing up with the leaders as I climbed down from the patrol car. Joey, Misty, Tory, Marcus, and I were going to the staging area in my Nova. Joey had decided that Marcus needed to be in our group, too.

"How did Garofalo like the plan?" I asked Joey.

Joey smiled. "I amended it slightly after I had that private word with him. Everyone heads out at the same time, boxes Fernandez in, and accepts any surrender that may come up."

We went inside the station. Marcus suddenly stopped in his tracks.

"What's wrong, Marcus?" asked Joey.

"I just had an awful thought," replied Marcus. "What if we're wrong about the men that Fernandez brought?"

"What do you mean?" asked Misty.

"What if they *aren't* just regular guys? Fernandez is a general in the Mexican army. Lots of those cartels use soldiers. It makes sense that Fernandez would, too," explained Marcus. "Hell, Felix Juarez carries the rank of colonel! What if we're leading a bunch of amateurs into a fight with professionals?"

Joey's face reflected the fact that he hadn't considered that possibility. He shared a look with Misty, then said, "So be it. They'll still be outnumbered. Maybe God'll give us a break on this one."

See? Just another layer on the shit cake.

"*Jefe,*" said Juarez. "Will you be addressing the men before we go?"

"*Si,*" replied Fernandez. He was applying fire to the crystal meth in his glass pipe. He inhaled deeply, and held the smoke. After a moment, he released it and coughed. "*En pocos minutos,* Felix. In a few minutes."

"They are loyal soldiers, Esteban."

Fernandez nodded as a smile crept along his face. "*Si.* They are." He inhaled again, then exhaled after holding it in for a moment. "Go, Felix. I will join you shortly, *amigo.*"

Juarez nodded and left the room.

Chapter 20

The other four went into the conference room. I ducked down to my office to pick up a couple of things.

"Hi, Mickey," said the man sitting in my visitor chair.

Manny Salazar was my partner years ago on the police force. Now, he was a private investigator. Manny was dressed in stained brown pants, beige shirt, and a mostly plain sport coat. The wrinkles in his clothes reminded me of a shar-pei. His overcoat was hanging on the hook that usually held my thin London Fog coat. It also had some unidentifiable stains.

"Manny, I really don't have time for you," I said, as I rifled my desk for my spare box of ammunition.

"Wow! That's a colorful lump on your head? What happened to you?

"Somebody dropped an apartment building on me. Or part of one."

"I saw all the rigmarole outside. What's going on?"

"Nothing that you need to know about, Manny."

"It's something big, isn't it?"

I found the box in the bottom drawer under some file folders. I pulled it out of the drawer and said, "It. Does. Not. Concern. You."

"Wow," said Manny. "Is that any way to treat the guy that saved your bacon with the Corn Flakes Killer?" He was shaking his head. "I only came by to see if you wanted to grab some dinner. My treat."

"Your treat? Let me guess...you either want something, or a rich uncle died and left you twenty dollars."

"I'm hurt. Do you think that little of me?"

"I think even less than that of you, Manny."

"To answer your question, a former client finally paid up for a divorce job I did for him about a year ago."

I started looking for my car keys. "That's nice, Manny."

"Yeah, he did own an apartment building on the corner of East Pershing and South Cottage Grove, not too far from the lake."

I started through desk drawers again. "That's great, Manny."

"The great part is that he sold the apartment building not too long ago. He sold it to a couple of really nice-dressed Mexican guys. Said one of them had a gray beard and never blinked. Creeped him out a little, but he sold it to them anyway. They paid cash, too, so he came and settled up with me."

I found my car keys in my middle desk drawer. They were beside the pencils. I grabbed them, put on my poor coat, and headed out the office door. "Bye, Manny."

"And you're still holding that bust from years ago against me, aren't you?"

I was halfway down the hall before I realized what Manny had said. I froze. Then, I started yelling for Joey and Marcus as I ran after Manny Salazar.

JOEY LEANED CLOSER to Manny and said, "Tell me again. What's your client's name?"

"Al Finch."

Joey leaned back to a seated position. "And what did he do?"

"Look, I'm not..."

Joey slammed his hand on the table. Everyone jumped. "I don't give a tinker's damn what you're 'not'! One thing you are 'not' is going anywhere until we find out what you know!"

"You can't talk to me like that, buddy! I used to be a cop. I know my rights inside and out!" shouted Manny.

Joey, now very calm, hands folded on the table in front of him, said, "Then you should know that those accused of being enemy combatants of the United States go away for long, long periods of time without being charged with a crime. Or, until it's deemed that they are no longer a threat." Joey stood up, leaned over the table into Manny's face, and quietly said, "I think you're an enemy combatant, Mr. Salazar. I think I need to ask Marcus here to send you to Guantanamo for a while. We'll even give you your own copy of the Koran. And your own waterboard."

Manny had a line of sweat across his forehead.

I kinda felt sorry for him. A little. Nah, he had this coming.

"Let me ask you one more time. Who is Al Finch, and what did he do?"

Manny gulped. "He was an old client of mine. I did some divorce work for him, and he stiffed me. Said he didn't have the money to pay me right away. That was a year ago."

Joey nodded, his face impassive. "And after that?"

"He came to my office and paid me what he owed me. He said that two Mexican guys bought the apartment building that he owned. He said they were nicely dressed, and that one had a gray beard and never blinked. He said they paid cash for the building."

"Did he give you any names?"

Manny shook his head. "No, he just mentioned it in passing. He was glad to be paying me off."

Joey slid his eyes to me. I nodded slightly, letting him know that I believed Manny. Marcus met my eyes, and deliberately closed one. I smiled slightly at the wink.

"Where is this Finch now, Salazar?"

Manny shook his head. "As far as I know, he was going to Florida. He had tickets for a cruise he was taking with some blond bimbo."

"And where is this apartment building?"

"Al said it was the corner of East Pershing and South Cottage."

"Misty, would you call that up on the map, please?"

Misty turned to the computer terminal that fed the projector. Her fingers flew across the keyboard. I was envious. I couldn't type worth shit.

On the wall, the photo of the apartment building popped up. Three stories, built within the last thirty years. Clean-looking. We studied it closely for a few minutes.

"Marcus," said Joey, "do you think that could hold a hundred or so people?"

"Easily," replied Marcus.

"Misty, what's around that building?" asked Joey.

Misty's fingers flew over the keyboard again, and the picture rotated around, displaying the buildings to the left and across the street.

As we studied the layout of the apartments and the buildings around it, Joey began to smile.

"Marcus, are you thinking what I'm thinking?"

"If you're thinking that we can surround this building with our people, instead of waiting for Fernandez in Burnham Park, then, yes, I'm thinking what you're thinking."

"We can catch Fernandez flat-footed! He won't know we've found his hiding place!"

Joey whirled around and pointed to Misty. "Sweetheart, get on the radio and call out to everyone. Have them unload quietly at least four blocks north of this place, all of them in the same place. Tell them not to be noticed. And I need to talk to Dexter."

Manny said, "Okay, you got what I had. Can I go now?"

Joey shook his head. "Not a chance in hell, Salazar. You're coming with us, mister."

"Like hell I am! You got nothing on me! Arrest me! I dare you!"

Marcus opened his badge case and showed it to Manny, while he sang "Cuban Pete".

"Looks like you're sitting on top of the shit cake, Manny," I said.

Manny glowered at me.

Joey decided that, since there were now six of us, we'd take the stealth helicopter.

ONCE WE WERE IN THE air, I said to Joey, "At least it's gotten dark. That should help."

Joey nodded. "It should."

"If I were Fernandez, I would have lookouts scattered around."

"I'm sure he does."

"Will it be a problem?"

Joey shook his head with a smile. "No, we have our own secret weapon against that."

No matter how I prodded, he wouldn't say any more.

I turned to Tory. He was staring out the window, fascinated by the scenery going by, and looking amazed at the lack of noise produced by the aircraft.

I turned to look at Manny. "How are you holding up, Manny?"

"This is pretty low, even for you, Mickey. I don't like getting drafted."

"I told you that it didn't concern you. Most people would have taken the hint and left."

"You could have told me this was Joey Justice, too."

"You didn't need to know."

"And telling them what Al Finch told me, that wasn't right."

I shrugged and held my hands wide. "Manny, the guy was your client. I had nothing to do with it."

Manny shook his head. "If this guy Fernandez that they're talking about is who I think it is, he don't forget stuff like this. Both of our asses may be firmly planted in some deep shit."

I nodded. "You're right, Manny. That's why we're doing what we're doing...so we can make that guy think twice about coming to Chicago. And if we catch him along the way, so much the better."

Manny shut his mouth and closed his eyes. We were landing.

Once the helicopter was settled, we climbed out. We had landed on a tennis court. A rough circle of people surrounded us, including Brandon, Patty, Louie, and Megan. Dexter met us as we came out of the aircraft.

"Any trouble with sentries, Dex?" asked Joey.

"Not on my part," replied Dex. "There were six on my side of the street. They're out of it. Fernandez is inside that building, all right." He paused. "Tony isn't back yet."

"You sure of that, sir?" said a voice behind us.

We whirled, and it was Tony. Over his shoulder, he carried an unconscious man. He eased the man to the ground.

"I think I got the raw end of the deal here," said Tony. "My side of the street, the guys had some training. I'm thinking Mexican Army...maybe some Special Forces. I brought this guy back to get some intel."

"Where did you put all the people, Dex?" asked Joey.

Dexter pointed down the street. "I found an empty building. Everyone's inside there. The buses are another four blocks further away."

Tony gave the man on the ground a vicious kick in the side of the leg. "Get *up*, asshole! I know you're awake, and I'm tired of carrying you!"

The man on the ground winced, then sat up slowly. "Owww," said the man, holding his head. He looked up at us, and held his hands out pleadingly. "*Por favor...no hablo Ingles!*"

Tony replied, "*No problemo, amigo. Hablo Espanol.* That one won't work. Might as well speak English."

The man on the ground glowered at Tony.

Joey said, "How many men does Fernandez have?"

"Who is Fernandez?" said the man, with a thick accent.

Tony delivered another vicious kick, this time to the man's side. "Try again, asshole."

"*Como se llama?*" asked Joey.

The man looked suspiciously at Joey. "Julio."

Joey nodded. "Julio, Fernandez isn't the only man capable of slow torture. Do you know who I am?"

Julio nodded. "*Si.* You are Joey Justice."

Joey smiled slightly. "Then you know that I'm not kidding. I'll cut off your testicles and make you eat them if you don't start talking to me now." Joey slowly drew a survival knife from a sheath beneath his shirt collar. He placed the point of the knife on Julio's cheek. "Or, I might just pluck one eye out of your head, and let you watch me burst it like a grape."

Julio swallowed, and looked frightened.

Joey pressed the point against the point of the man's cheekbone, almost drawing blood. "So...let's try again. How many men does Fernandez have with him inside that building?" Joey very gently let the knife point puncture the man's cheek slightly.

Tory turned away. I felt a churning in my stomach, too.

Julio, staring into Joey's eyes, whispered, "One hundred and eighteen."

"Who are they, Julio? Are they Mexican Army?"

"*Si.*"

"How did Fernandez get them to Chicago?" asked Joey.

"From the lake, *senor.*"

"What ship?" asked Joey, still pressing the knife against Julio's cheek.

"Fuck you," said Julio, and drove his head forward hard enough to drive Joey's knife into his brain.

"Shit!" yelled Joey, jumping back.

I gasped with surprise, and so did most of our circle.

Julio fell over onto the tennis court. He was dead.

Tony delivered one more hard, vicious kick to Julio. "Coward!" he yelled, as the kick found its mark. Tony pulled Joey's knife out of Julio's face, wiped it clean on Julio's clothes, and handed it back to Joey.

Joey took the knife and sheathed it behind his collar again.

I looked around. "Where's Manny?"

"You mean this guy?" asked Louie. He came up to our group, with Manny in a headlock. "I caught him tryin' to sneak past us. Figured he belonged to you guys." Louie set Manny on his feet.

Manny saw the dead man lying on the tennis court.

"Oh, man, the shitstorm's started!" said Manny.

"Manny, you need to stay with us," I said.

Joey slowly walked over to Manny, and put his face within a couple of inches of Manny's. "Yeah, Manny. You make a guy feel like you don't want his company. That true, Manny?"

Manny, to his credit, wouldn't let Joey intimidate him. "No, Justice, I just don't want anything to do with Esteban Fernandez. I'm not a cop anymore, and I'm not getting paid for this."

Still two inches from Manny's face, Joey asked, "Mickey?"

"Joey?"

"This guy any good?"

Grudgingly, I said, "Yeah. He can be."

After a pause, Joey said, "Manny, I'll pay you five grand to fight with us."

Manny, smiling, reached out and shook Joey's hand. "Why didn't you say so, partner? Glad to be part of this!"

Chapter 21

"Felix! Come here!" called Fernandez.

The door opened, and Juarez stepped inside. "*Si, Jefe?*"

Fernandez was checking his appearance in the mirror. As he straightened his tie and put on his suit coat, he said, "I will address the men now. It is almost time to go to the park."

Juarez nodded. "*Si, Jefe.*"

As Juarez began to leave the room, a voice from a loudspeaker outside could be heard inside the third floor apartment.

"Fernandez! Esteban Fernandez! This is Joey Justice!" Pause. "Wanna come out and play?"

Juarez locked eyes with Fernandez.

"*Madre de dios!*" said Juarez, as both men bolted from the room.

JOEY PRESSED THE BUILT-in button on the megaphone and said, "Fernandez! I'm here! You've said you wanted me, now here's your chance! Come out, and we'll settle our differences man-to-man!" He lowered the megaphone.

"Baby, I don't think he's listening," said Misty, into Joey's ear.

"Oh, he's listening, all right," replied Joey.

"WE MAY BE SURROUNDED inside this building, but do I show concern?" said Fernandez. He was addressing his men. "No, I do not. That is because I know you are the best men that my army has to offer." He stopped, and his face was no longer smiling. His eyes were wide, and his face was a rictus. He was not blinking, and the resemblance to a shark's smile was stronger than ever. "You will go out every opening in this building! You will swarm as if you were angry hornets! *You will kill my enemies and bring to me Joey Justice! You will bring me his head separated from his body!*" He was breathing heavily. "*You will kill him! Now, take your positions! When I give the order, you will storm out of this building!*"

JOEY PRESSED THE MEGAPHONE button again. "Fernandez! I'm waiting for you! Have you turned into a coward?" He lowered the megaphone, and turned to Mickey. "I think he's actually afraid to come out."

As Joey finished the sentence, men dressed in camouflage uniforms burst from every opening in the building, and began firing automatic weapons.

With bullets flying all around him, Joey yelled into the megaphone, "*Fire! FIRE! Return fire!*" He then began taking his own advice, and started firing back, murmuring swear words with every shot he fired.

Hand grenades began exploding around the area, as members of the Fernandez gang threw them at Joey's surrounding army. From the roof of the building, a white contrail erupted, and an RPG exploded behind Joey's position.

Joey got onto his radio and said, "Use everything we have! Fire it all! Take these guys out!"

And, with that order, the sound of the battle rang through the streets of the East Side.

MEGAN BECK, POSITIONED in front of the apartment building, was shooting at anything in front of her that moved. She had machine guns in each hand, and the straps for each were around her neck and shoulders. Her biceps bulged as she fought the recoil produced by the weapons. She was screaming, "*YAHHHHH!*" at the top of her voice, and didn't realize it.

As the members of the Mexican Army tried to find cover from her maddened fire, Megan put the guns aside so that she could lob a couple of hand grenades at the fighting Mexicans. She then took a grenade, and, with a windup like a professional baseball pitcher, she threw one directly into the door of the building. It bounced twice inside the door and exploded, injuring several men still inside the building.

Megan was the point of a triangle. The other corners were Dexter and Louie, and both were firing weapons as fast as they could to eliminate the threat that they were facing.

Others were spread out behind them, in a staggered skirmish line. They were advancing across the street, facing down the bullets that were coming their way. When someone was hit, they dropped down, and another person took their place.

Miriam Apple was inside the building across the street, along with Steve, her cameraman. They were filming everything that happened, and Miriam was providing a running commentary. Steve, a former U. S. Army Ranger, couldn't stand any more. He saw his veteran friend, Tony Armstrong, barely miss getting shot. He handed Miriam the camera and looked into her eyes.

Miriam knew that he was about to join Joey's people against Fernandez. "Be careful, Steve."

Steve nodded an acknowledgement, and ran outside to pick up a weapon.

Megan began razing the front of the building, working her way from the first floor to the third floor. No windows were unbroken. She stopped firing for a moment, watching the roof. Finally, a head popped up to take a look, and Megan was ready. The man's head exploded from the force of Megan's shot.

Finally, three Mexican Army men were left in front of the building. They threw down their guns and raised their hands in surrender.

Taking her radio, Megan transmitted to anyone else that was listening. "The front of the building is secure."

Louie and Dexter had the prisoners in custody. She turned to help the wounded, and instructed the people that were in her group to do what they could.

Sirens could be heard in the distance.

ON THE NORTH SIDE OF the building, there wasn't much room. There was a small parking lot, a small street, and then, another apartment building. Most members of the police contingent, while sporadically scattered throughout the circle enclosing the building, were on this side, along with Jessica Queen.

When the battle erupted, Jessica kept a close watch on Petrie and his partner. If her suspicions were at all correct, Petrie's partner would soon attempt to contact Fernandez.

Jessica wished Charlie Li were beside her. Every time they worked together, Charlie always had her back. She never had to check.

She had a couple of grunts backing her on this side, but they weren't Charlie.

Everyone was firing weapons. Petrie's partner was even firing into the Mexicans, and had dropped several of them.

Had their suspicions been wrong?

From her position behind a concrete barrier, Jessica occasionally popped up, took aim, and fired shots at the criminals.

She noticed that Petrie had somehow gotten behind his partner. As she watched, Petrie aimed his weapon at his partner's head, and pulled the trigger!

Shocked, Jessica ran to stop the rogue cop. Before she could get to him, he had shot two other cops.

Jessica drew her handgun and aimed at Petrie. Bullets were still flying around her as she took her stance. Petrie was aiming his weapon at Sam Tanner. With no time to spare, Jessica fired one shot. Petrie's head jerked forward, and he dropped. Tanner whirled around at the commotion, saw Jessica, and immediately figured out what happened. He waved his thanks to her, as she dropped back down behind a small stone fence.

As Jessica became aware again of the people around her, she noticed that she was crouched beside Captain Baker.

"Good job, Miss Queen," said the captain.

Jessica smiled slightly. "Thank you, Captain."

Radios held by both Jessica and Captain Baker came to life at that moment. It was Megan, saying that the front was under control.

"I hope she's pleased with herself," said Jessica. She aimed at a Mexican Army soldier, and shot him just before he could lob a grenade at one of the police's places of cover. The early November darkness kept the other soldiers from seeing that he dropped it. It exploded, killing or injuring the few soldiers still fighting.

Two soldiers suddenly raised their hands in surrender. Captain Baker held his handgun over his head, signifying to the police to cease fire.

With a smirk, Jessica spoke into her own radio. "North side secure."

As the officers spread out to assist the injured, the captain looked at Jessica. "You enjoyed saying that, didn't you?"

Still smirking, Jessica said, "Righto I did." She walked over to Sam and helped him up from the cold asphalt. "You all right, Sam?"

Sam nodded. "I'm fine. But I could sure use something to eat right now."

ON THE BACK SIDE OF the apartment building, the fighting was led by Rizzo, with Garofalo helping. Some of the people that came with Timothy Taylor were back here, too, but Tim himself was with Joey, Mickey, and Manny.

Back here, Rizzo and Garofalo were the only two men with radios.

For several minutes, the fighting was fast and furious. Several of Garofalo's men were killed, and many more were injured.

Finally, the fighting ended. There were no members of the Mexican Army still standing on the back side of the apartment building.

Rizzo saw that Garofalo was about to give the all-clear on the radio. He yelled at the crime leader. "Hey, Garofalo, c'mere! Hurry!"

Garofalo tucked the radio into his coat pocket without giving an all-clear. When he got to Rizzo, he said, "What's up, Rizzo?"

"You remember when you and Mickey was workin' for Tony the Knife?"

"Yeah, so what?"

Rizzo chuckled. "Mickey says he was seein' this girl. She'd been a hooker." Rizzo pointed at Garofalo. "Mickey said you killed her over nuthin'...a bag of pot or somethin'. You told Mickey, 'Big deal, she was a whore.' Remember that?"

"She *was* just a whore."

Rizzo, nodding, chuckled again. "Not anymore, she wasn't. She was givin' it up for Mickey. Her name was Tanya. Mickey asked her to marry him, and she said yes. Then you killed her." Rizzo's face went blank. "Mickey didn't forget.

He said that if you survived Fernandez, that I was to make things right." He drew his handgun. "Sorry, Pietro. But this one is personal. For Mickey...and for Tanya."

Rizzo shot Garofalo in the head, then shot him again after he fell to the ground.

Rizzo put his gun in its holster, and looked down at Garofalo for a moment. He took out his radio.

"Everything's clear in the back. Bad news – Garofalo didn't make it."

He put the radio back into his pocket, then went to finish off any Mexicans that were still alive.

"*Jefe,* we must go! Now! While we can still get out!" said Juarez.

"*No!* I will not run away from him!" shouted Fernandez.

"If you do not, Esteban, he will either kill us or capture us! We must go!"

Fernandez, blind with anger, drew a handgun and put it against Juarez' head. "We...will...*fight,* Felix!"

Calmly, Juarez said, "Then we will die, Esteban. If that is what you choose, then, it will be so."

Fernandez was fighting the battle inside. Juarez could see it in his eyes. Finally, Fernandez uttered, "Arrgh!" He put away his weapon and said, "How can we escape?"

Juarez pointed to two dead Chicago patrolmen on the floor just inside the building, beside one of the windows.

A BULLET RICOCHETED off of the curb in front of Joey. He was using the median curb for cover.

On the south side of the building, only six Mexican Army soldiers were still fighting. The rest were either dead or injured so badly that they couldn't fight anymore.

Tim Taylor and a couple of others were attempting to sneak up behind the soldiers, while Mickey, Misty, and Tory were sneaking up from the other side.

Joey keyed the megaphone again. "*Dejen sus armas!* Put down your weapons, and you won't be harmed!"

Two more shots zinged off of the curb in front of him. He thought to himself, *There's your answer, Justice!*

Four shots – *tap, tap,* and then, *tap, tap* - rang out.

Suddenly, four soldiers had their hands in the air, and were surrendering to Tim.

It was over. At least, with the soldiers.

Joey spoke into his radio. "Anyone see Fernandez or Juarez?"

No one answered in the affirmative.

Dammit!

Nobody registered that two uniformed cops were walking away to the northeast.

At first.

"Hey, Joey!" called Mickey.

"Yeah!" answered Joey.

Mickey pointed at the two cops in the distance. "Aren't those two a little short to be on the Chicago force?"

Joey looked. Realization crossed his face. "Holy shit!" He yelled into his radio. "Somebody stop those two! That's *him!*" He began running after them.

Fernandez and Juarez looked back. Patty Ferguson was closing in on them. Fernandez pulled his gun and shot her.

Patty fell to the ground.

Brandon King fired an entire clip at the two fake policemen.

The two criminals kept running in the direction of the 31st Street Harbor. Joey was at least a block behind them, followed closely by Tory Masterson and Mickey Rooney.

Chapter 22

I ran. I ran as hard as I could.

Tory soon left me behind, and Joey was way out ahead of both of us.

My almost-healed leg wouldn't let me run any faster.

As I ran, I kept telling myself that my leg was healed. And if it wasn't healed, it was still good enough to keep running. And if I was falling behind, it wasn't because my leg wasn't healed – it was only because Joey and Tory could run faster than I could. I told myself that there was no pain.

Then I told myself that I was full of fertilizer.

I soon realized that someone was running along beside me. When I saw who it was, I had the shock of my life.

It was Manny Salazar.

My ex-partner.

He was keeping up with me, and wasn't even breathing hard.

Bastard.

"Why are you running with me, Manny?" I asked between gasps of air.

"I'm hurt. I still care about you, Mickey. I figure I can keep your ass in one piece if I go along with you."

I was limping so badly at that point that it couldn't even be considered running.

"Manny," I said, "if you really want to help me, run ahead and help Joey and Tory. I'll catch up."

"Why should I help them?"

"Five grand, remember?"

"Oh, yeah! Good reason. Okay, you got it." He started jogging in the direction that the others were heading. "But you're buying dinner!"

I waved him on as I tried to catch my breath. After a few seconds of breathing heavily, I began jogging again, pressing hard on my sore leg.

Manny was already out of sight.

Bastard.

FERNANDEZ AND JUAREZ had reached the harbor docks.

Joey saw them duck into the maze of cargo crates, barrels, and shacks on the dock itself. He slowed down to catch his breath.

Tory caught up to him. He had his department-issued .38 in his hand. "Okay, Joey, where are they?"

Joey pointed. "They went there."

Both men were still breathing heavily.

"What do you want to do?" asked Tory.

Joey shook his head. "Only thing we can do." He pointed. "You go that way, and I'll go this way." They began moving onto the pier. Joey stopped. "Tory, I want him alive, if at all possible."

"So do I. He's got a lot to answer for."

The two men began making their way slowly around the packing crates that were stacked on the dock.

"ESTEBAN, THEY ARE COMING."

"*Si.* Have you radioed to Manuel?"

"*Si, Jefe.* He is entering the harbor now. He will be here in moments."

"*Muy bueno.* We must leave this place."

Juarez caught a glimpse of someone. It wasn't a clear glimpse, because of the darkness and the shadows on the pier, but the person was about fifty feet away.

"I see someone, Esteban."

Fernandez nodded and waved. "Go, Felix. But hurry."

Juarez began moving stealthily along the packing crates. He came to an opening between crates, and stepped quietly into it, intending to go around the crates and silently catch the man that he had spotted.

Fernandez was watching warily in the direction that Juarez had gone. He froze when the voice came from behind him.

"Fernandez."

Fernandez whirled around with his handgun in his hand, but Joey was expecting that move. He knocked the gun to the pier, and it skidded across the boards and into the water of Lake Michigan.

Joey followed with a right cross to Fernandez' left eye, which also slid across Fernandez' face, broke his nose, and knocked him to the boards.

"Get up, you son of a bitch, so I can give you the ass-kicking you deserve," said Joey. Then, Joey saw nothing but stars...and blackness.

MANNY GOT TO THE PIER just in time to see Juarez slip to the corner of some crates, pull his hand back, and appear to hit something.

Manny skidded to a stop. He could still see Juarez' leg. Knowing that only Joey or Tory would have been hit from behind by Juarez, Manny took careful aim with his .44.

"THANK YOU, FELIX! Now, *kill him!*" screamed Fernandez.

"*Si.*" Juarez took careful aim.

BLAM!

Felix Juarez spun around, fell, and dropped his handgun. The gun was quickly lost in the darkness. A neat, round hole was on both sides of Juarez' left calf, and both holes were bleeding.

Behind them, at the edge of the pier, something broke through the surface of the water.

It was a Marlin six-person submarine.

The hatch of the submarine opened, and a Hispanic man was shouting at Fernandez. "*Jefe! Jefe! Prisa! Andele! Prisa!*"

Juarez stood on his good leg, and began limping to the sub. Fernandez looked at the submarine, then looked at Joey, helpless on the dock.

Behind Fernandez, two shots were fired, and holes appeared in the packing crate inches from Fernandez' head. Fernandez ducked, and with an inarticulate scream of frustration, ran toward the submarine. Behind him, Tory fired two more shots. Both ricocheted off of the pier, then Fernandez followed Juarez inside, screaming, "*Sumergirse, Manuel! Sumergirse!*"

The hatch closed, and the submarine began diving just as Manny got within firing range. He fired two rounds at the submerged underwater boat, but the bullets went harmlessly into the waters of Lake Michigan.

Esteban Fernandez was gone.

I GOT TO THE PIER JUST as Manny was firing into the water after the submarine.

I limped over to Joey just as Tory got to him.

"Tell me he's not dead," I said.

"He would have been, if I hadn't shot one of those assholes in the leg," said Manny. "It looked like one of them hit Joey on the head from behind. I think that bastard was lining up a shot when I shot him."

Tory nodded, as he check Joey's pulse. "It looked like Fernandez still wanted to hurt him, but, by then, I was shooting at him, too. The submarine took me by surprise." He looked up at me. "His pulse is strong and steady, but that's twice he's been knocked on the head...and in less than twenty-four hours. We need to get him to a hospital."

I pulled out my encrypted radio and pressed the "transmit" button. "Marcus Moore, do you copy?"

"This is Marcus, Mickey. Where are you? What's happening?"

"Marcus, we're at the pier at the 31st Street Harbor. Joey's unconscious. Looks like Juarez hit him on the head with something. We need an ambulance."

"Copy that, Mickey. Fernandez?"

I took a breath. "Fernandez escaped in a submarine, Marcus." Manny told me what it was. "A small Marlin submarine. He's gone."

There was a pause. "Copy that. Ambulance is on its way...with an almost frantic woman aboard."

Misty. I smiled. "Copy, Marcus. Could you send us a ride, too? We're on foot, and all out of 'run'."

I could hear the smile in his voice. "Copy."

MISTY ARRIVED RIDING inside the ambulance. Before the wheels stopped turning, she opened the back doors, jumped out, and ran to Joey's side.

"He's okay, Misty, just out. Apparently, Juarez hit him in the head with something. Manny shot Juarez before he could do anything else."

Misty ran her hand over Joey's head very lightly, felt the bump on the back of his head, and winced. Then she stood, walked over to Manny, and looked into his eyes.

"Thank you," she said, with simple sincerity. She then stood on tiptoe and kissed Manny on the cheek. Surprisingly, Manny blushed.

Misty returned to Joey's side, and climbed into the ambulance after the paramedics loaded him. The doors closed, and Joey was hauled off to the hospital.

Two patrol cars pulled up to the pier as the ambulance drove away. Marcus got out of one of them.

His eyes went from me, to Tory, and to Manny. Then he nodded once.

"Nice job, people."

Chapter 23

The news reports called it a gang war. Of course, we dropped hints that that was exactly what it was, and that it was over. The reporters bought it.

One newsperson knew the whole story, though. But, Joey's reporter friend, Miriam Apple, decided to keep quiet about the story.

"If I tell the world about this one, then some other troublesome asshole will bring his line of shit to Chicago, bragging about how much better he is than Fernandez." She shook her head. "No, I'm not empowering anybody else. What the public doesn't know won't hurt you, Lieutenant."

Miriam then gave to Joey the digital recording that she had made. Then she turned to Steve. "You asshole. You're determined to get yourself killed, aren't you?"

Steve shrugged, and the two TV people left.

I was grateful.

The final tally was one hundred and thirty one dead, mostly Mexican Army soldiers. Seventeen of the dead were cops. Joey had lost seven grunts.

The surviving members of Fernandez' army were whisked away somewhere. I never found out where, but, I never asked, either.

Joey was kept overnight in the hospital for observation. Misty stayed by his side all night long. Finally, the doctors released him, declaring that his head was made of some previously unknown metal alloy that doesn't dent.

Patty Ferguson had been shot in the shoulder, but the bulletproof vest she had worn took most of the impact, and had left major bruises. She was also treated and released, much to the relief of Brandon King.

Marcus spent one last night helping me forget what had happened.

Sam decided that all of that shooting had made him hungry, and that only a big cheeseburger from Bradley's Burger Barn would satisfy him.

Manny's client, Al Finch, was found floating in the Des Plaines River. He had been shot in the head. Fernandez must have thought that the man told the police about the apartment building.

The submarine that Fernandez had escaped in was found in Georgian Bay, on the Canadian side of Lake Huron. The sub had gone undetected through the Straits of Mackinac, over to the Canadian side. No trace was found of Fernandez, Juarez, or the sub driver. From there, they could have gone anywhere.

Dexter said that Fernandez would turn up again, especially since Joey had broken Fernandez' nose. He said that pride wouldn't let Fernandez leave that alone.

Dexter and Megan supervised the repacking of the equipment they had brought. It wasn't long before the conference room was back to normal.

The day that Justice Security was leaving Chicago for the return home, Dexter pulled me off to the side.

"Mickey, do you remember Charlie Li?" asked Dexter.

"Of course I do!"

Dexter smiled. "He married Carly Stewart."

I shook my head and said, "May God help that poor man."

Dexter laughed and said, "May God help Justice Security when he comes home with her."

Rizzo and his remaining cohorts had flown home earlier that morning. Joey had a second Justice Security private jet come to the airport to take Rizzo and the gang home.

I overheard Joey talking to Rizzo. "Listen, tell Mickey he has my gratitude. And thank you for your help, Rizzo. I knew I could count on you."

Rizzo smiled a lopsided smile at Joey. "Hey, you're welcome. Glad I could help, Joey. Be seein' ya."

Joey smiled back. "Tell Mickey to keep his nose clean."

Marcus had asked me to find Tim Taylor and Manny, and to have them at the District that afternoon. I found them, and brought them. Marcus, Tim, Manny, Sam, Tory, Joey, Misty, Louie, Jessica, Dexter, Megan and I were all once more in the conference room, along with Captain Baker.

Marcus said, "Before we leave for home, I have something for all of you. You won't be able to brag about it for a long time, if ever...but it's yours as long as you keep it secret. Timothy Taylor, will you please step forward?"

Tim, looking puzzled, stepped over to Marcus.

"Mr. Taylor, it is with great pleasure that I present to you this check, along with this Presidential Commendation, for your services in assisting us with eliminating the Fernandez threat from the city of Chicago. It's signed by the big man himself." He handed Tim two envelopes, and shook his hand.

It turned out that Marcus had Presidential Commendations and tax-free checks for all of us.

Except for Tory.

Tory Masterson got something in addition to his check and commendation.

"Detective First Grade Tory Masterson," said Marcus. "I formally offer you a position with the FBI, in my office, under my authority, with pay reflecting your position as Special Agent. The only codicil is that you have to move to our city. Is this something you'd be interested in accepting?"

Tory's face broke into a huge smile, and his eyes widened. "You bet I would, sir! I mean, I'll have to talk it over with my wife, but I'm sure she'll be as happy as I am to accept! Thank you, Mr. Moore!"

Marcus smiled. "You'll have to pass through training at Quantico, but, after that, you'll be in my office. You can even help me out with *these* bozos, if you'd like." He had pointed his thumb at the Justice Security people.

"You're *on*, Chief!" said Tory.

"Uh, excuse me?" said Joey. "Bozos?" He stood up straight. "At least, I broke Fernandez' nose. I think that rates me better than bozo."

"Shoulda shot the asshole, Joey," said Louie quietly. "Woulda put you in the 'stooge' category then."

Everyone laughed.

Then, one by one, they said goodbye to Captain Baker, Manny, Sam, and I.

Joey stopped at Manny, and looked him in the eye. "I owe my life to you, Mr. Salazar. Thank you."

"Ah, you're in good company," said Manny, throwing a thumb toward me. "Seems like I'm saving everybody's bacon lately."

Joey stopped to thank me, too. "You're welcome to come visit anytime, Michelle. I'd offer you a partnership right now, but I get the feeling that you wouldn't accept."

I smiled and shook my head. "Nah. I'm okay here. But I might take you up on that visit sometime."

All of Justice Security had left the room except for Marcus. He took my hand in both of his, then lifted it to his lips. "I'm sorry it can't be more for us than it was, Mickey."

"So am I." I shrugged. "I guess it just wasn't meant to be."

"Thank you."

"Thank *you*, Marcus. Stay safe."

Marcus turned to leave.

"Oh, wait, Marcus! I have a request!"

"What is it, Mickey?"

"I'd like to request that two agents, Carter and Young, be transferred to Alaska somewhere. If you're feeling generous."

Smiling and laughing, Marcus turned to the door, and with a wave, he was gone.

Captain Baker looked at Sam and me. "You two are off duty for a minimum of two days."

"But, Captain, I've got..." I started.

The captain held up his hand. "I don't want to hear it. Out. Two days. That's an order."

Tim and Sam walked with Manny and me down to my office. As we passed the station entrance, Tim said that he would see me at Milt's, and left. Sam left with him.

Manny followed me to my office.

"How about that dinner, Mickey?"

"What dinner?"

"You know perfectly well what dinner."

I picked up my coat and put it on. "Where were you thinking?"

"Let me surprise you."

"God help me."

YOU'RE READY FOR BOOK 9 in the *Justice Security* series: *Jim Dandy – A Justice Security Novel.*

It's available at your favorite eBook seller.

About The Author: T. M. Bilderback is a former radio announcer with a number of story ideas running around inside his head, most based on or inspired by classic songs. The author currently resides in Tennessee, and is writing feverishly in order to banish these stories from his head and into book form before he runs screaming into the street.

Other works by T. M. Bilderback

N<u>*icholas Turner*</u>
 If You Could Read My Mind
<u>*Justice Security*</u>
Mama Told Me Not To Come
Someone Saved My Life Tonight
Jackie Blue
Wake Me Up Before You Go-Go
Saturday In The Park
MacArthur Park
The Little Drummer Boy
The Night Chicago Died
Jim Dandy
Cow Patty
Hell's Bells
<u>*Tales Of Sardis County*</u>
Don't Come Around Here No More
Junior's Farm
The Devil's In The Details
I'm Your Boogie Man
<u>*Colonel Abernathy's Tales*</u>
The Lion Sleeps Tonight
Heart Of Glass
<u>*Other Stories*</u>
The Wreck Of The Edmund Fitzgerald
Gold
Hot Child In The City
Eli's Coming
<u>*Other Novels*</u>
Empty Eyes
<u>*Short Story Collections*</u>
Greatest Hits